Will I Ever Know

W9-CUQ-463

Charles Henry

Outskirts Press, Inc.
Denver, Colorado

Outskirts Press, Inc.
http://www.outskirtspress.com

ISBN: 978-1-4327-2092-6

Outskirts Press and the "OP" logo are trademarks belonging to Outskirts Press, Inc.

PRINTED IN THE UNITED STATES OF AMERICA

Dedication

This novel is lovingly dedicated to Frances Langford, Singer, Film Star, Artist, Patriot, and overall "Good Guy."

Frances spent many years of her life touring and entertaining our armed forces in remote places in the world. Bringing them some respite as they fought for our freedom. Bringing them a sense of home, family, and the life they had left behind.

She was at the same time mother, sister, girlfriend, and wife to all of them. Her newspaper column in WWII, "Purple Heart Diary" for the Hearst newspapers, brought to the homeland news and insights into what our forces were going through overseas.

Her renditions of "I'm in the Mood for Love" and "Moonglow" are legend, as are her many other great recordings.

The movies that she starred in, such as *The Bamboo Blond*, *Beat the Band* with Gene Krupa, *Career Girl*, and *Swing It Soldier* show her to be a wonderful, warm actress with tremendous appeal, lighting up the screen with her beautiful smile. She appeared on radio and early TV in a very successful sitcom, *The Bickersons*, with Don Ameche.

Frances unofficially retired around 1957. The music scene had changed drastically. The demand for her style had waned. She did do some television, mostly as a guest star, and she did tour again during the Vietnam war, bringing the same joy and peace to those fighting forces as she had to their fathers twenty years earlier.

Frances had no regrets; she said in interviews that the most rewarding part of her career was the time she spent entertaining the troops. It is hoped that this book will motivate people to seek out Frances on CD, DVD, VHS, and mp3 formats.

Once you experience Frances Langford, she will remain forever in your heart.

Soli Deo Gloria

Acknowledgements

First of all, I'd like to thank my wife, Priscilla Henry, for all of her love, patience, and support for *Will I Ever Know*. Her untiring efforts at research lend authenticity to the various time-periods of the book. Without her hard work and dedication, *Will I Ever Know* would have remained just a dream.

I'd like to thank my Aunt Betty and Uncle Frank Prybyla for their support, encouragement, and their insight.

Also, I'd like to thank Joe Castellino for his enthusiasm and support from the beginning, when *Will I Ever Know* was just an idea.

Also, thank-you's go out to John Sweet and Joe Embery for their advice and suggestions.

Many thanks to Millissa Probart of Outskirts Press for her enthusiasm, support, and help through the process, and her tireless willingness to answer all of my many questions.

Also, a big thank you to the Outskirts Press team for their hard work and professionalism throughout the journey.

I would also like to thank GOD for giving me the story and for filling my mind with fresh ideas every morning.

Part I
Introduction

Chapter 1
Chad Henson

My name is Chad Henson—34-years-old, divorced, unemployed, and I'm in love with a dead woman. I was born in Philadelphia Pa. July 20th 1973. My parents were ex-hippies who traded their peace signs and love beads for a solid middle-class life and values. We weren't poor but we weren't rich either. My father had a variety of jobs, finally ending up with a good, indoor position at the main post office. My mother was mostly a stay-at-home mom, but she did do some part-time work for a temp service, doing mostly clerical work.

I was an only child, spoiled I admit. I was also a daydreamer. When I should have been concentrating on English grammar, mathematical equations, and the events surrounding the Battle of Hastings, I was off on some "adventure" in the movies or television romancing all the starlets. I managed to graduate from high school, but all I ever wanted was a career in show business. This, of course, led me nowhere but to the stock room of the local Value Barn discount department store.

I flirted with junior college, taking a course here and there but with nothing solid in mind. My aunt and uncle encouraged me to go to the community college and take a liberal arts course. But I was a conservative and was suspicious of anything called "liberal."

I did advance to being supervisor of the jewelry dept. at Value Barn. Big title, small raise in pay. I didn't break my back working, always maintaining a delicate balance between sloth and inactivity.

I dated sporadically, never having a steady girl for very long. A pattern had developed. I'd take a girl to the movies, fall in love with the female star, end up never wanting to see the girl I was with again.

I did go steady with a girl from the Value Barn, Cheryl Bickwell, for a little under two years. But after the first six months we did nothing but have small skirmishes and huge fights. I think we stayed together because neither one of us had any other prospects. I wanted to break it off, but we both worked at the same Value Barn and I didn't think the tension would be beneficial to either one of us.

The straw that broke "Chad's" back happened on my 28th birthday. Cheryl took me out to a restaurant called Flamin' Raymonds near the store. The meal passed rather calmly and pleasantly. Cheryl went on and on about the people she didn't like at Value Barn. They were all out to "get" her. She droned on and on while my mind was a million miles away. A birthday present to myself was not having to go anywhere with her after dinner.

I made up some sort of excuse that there was to be a family gathering later for my birthday. Not caring much for my family, there was no pressure from Cheryl to be included. The feeling was mutual, by the way. My family didn't care for her very much either.

After dinner, in the parking lot, she gave me a birthday present. I opened it up, trying to be appreciative and enthusiastic. It turned out to be a perfectly awful shirt, with what I perceived to be a "strange aroma" attached to it. Also attached to it were the remnants of a Value Barn price tag. It was a white short sleeve shirt that had all sorts of geometric shapes and clashing colors. It gave me a slight case of vertigo looking at it. The first word that came to mind was "hideous."

"Thank you SO much for this beautiful, wonderful shirt," I gushed, not wanting to cause a fight on my birthday. Being a frustrated actor, I gave my best academy award performance. She replied, acidly, "Well, I didn't know what to get you, you're so hard to buy for, you're not like other men, you don't have any hobbies."

That was it. I took the shirt, threw it in the trunk of the car, and took off. Happy birthday, Chad. I never talked to her again. It wasn't just that comment. This had been building for a long time. I was sick of her belittling comments. I was sick of her. As far as us both working at Value Barn, a month after the "shirt" incident, she transferred to a store in the northern suburbs. My loss was their gain............HAH!

I wanted to get married. I wanted to marry Thalia, the Latin pop star, or Anna Netrebko, the Russian opera singer, but it didn't look like hooking up with either one was going to happen—very soon anyway. Besides, they were both already married. Also, there might be a communication problem in both cases.

Then I met Feliccia Christianson, Philadelphia police detective. Feliccia was a gorgeous redhead, medium build. Not only was she beautiful, she was also kind and even-tempered. But I was told that on the job, a tougher cop did not exist.

She came into the store looking for a special kind of brooch. We got talking, and it turned out she liked old movies, big band swing, and jazz. We didn't see all that much of each other due to the irregularity of her job, but six months later we were married in Oct. of 2000.

Having both been "bachelors" for so long, marriage was a big adjustment for both of us. She had a lovely 2br apartment in the northeast part of Philadelphia, so I moved in after we were married. It was supposed to be only temporary while we looked for a house. Even after marriage, I continued keeping my delicate balance between sloth and inactivity. Feliccia, on the other hand, was very ambitious, and was looking to get ahead. She worked long hours with lots of overtime. She made way more money than I did, but I didn't care; I was happy she was so happy with her job, always getting awards and commendations.

In the spring of 2005, Feliccia told me that she was taking a job, for a lot more money, in Seattle, Washington, and that she was..............going alone. An old friend, Harry Parker, had put in a good word for her. I was shocked, but not really surprised. We both moved out, Feliccia to Seattle and me to a 1br apartment in a more "affordable" area.

In the fall of 2005, Value Barn was bought by Amalgamated Marketing Inc. Amalgamated owned several chains of discount department stores, such as Shopwell, Discountdaze, Betties Basement, Bargainz 4U, and others. Several of the Value Barn stores would become Bargainz 4U. A couple of stores in the city would become Betties Basement. My store would be called "Out of Business."

Charles Henry

The employees of the renamed stores would be rehired. Amalgamated held a big meeting for the employees of the stores that would be closing. At the meeting, they asked for a show of hands of those who wished to continue working for the new company. Almost everyone raised their hands, me included. I was one of the first to be let go. Over ten years of loyal faithful service............out the window.

I now had more time to indulge in my "hobbies." Yes, Cheryl, I do have hobbies! Watching—and I stress "watching"—sports, movies, especially old movies, listening to all kinds of music. I'm the definition of what President Kennedy called a "spectator."

One day in the early spring of 2006, while going through some CDs that Feliccia had left behind, I spotted one of Frances Langford. I had heard of her, knowing only that she had done a radio show that later became a hit on early TV with Don Ameche called *The Bickersons*. But that was situation comedy. I thought of Frances as a comedienne, and here was a CD of her singing some great old songs. I thought this might be good for a laugh so I popped it into the CD player.

"Someone to Watch Over Me"—hmmm, that's a good place to start, one of my favorite old songs. What I heard completely overwhelmed me! This gal could really SING! I went through the whole CD, all the songs. Those I knew and those I didn't know. WOW, I couldn't believe it! I got onto the computer and did a search for "Frances Langford."

I found out that not only was she a singer, but she'd made over 30 feature films, most in starring roles. That she was a regular on Bob Hope's radio show. Had her own radio show and was a guest star on countless radio and TV programs. Also, that she'd spent years touring with Hope's USO show entertaining the troops in WWII, Korea, and Vietnam, and had died at age 92 in 2005. The pictures that filled these websites were of Frances in her prime in the 1940's and showed an absolutely drop-dead gorgeous blond with a smile that could charm the vilest creature.

But it was the "VOICE" that really had my attention. I had never heard anything like it. Light and airy yet able to be dark and steamy, with a tone that was as clear as a mountain stream. I began to search and found that there were at least six other CDs of Frances available. I also found VHS and DVDs of some of her movies. I eagerly ordered all I could find. I was able to tape several of her movies from the classics channel. I was officially a "fan."

Will I Ever Know

It wasn't long before I was able to boldly declare that Frances Langford had "the most beautiful voice I'd ever heard." Period………………….. I also ordered many of her photos online. Those I didn't hang up, I put in a scrapbook along with movie posters, articles, and such. I was becoming obsessed with Frances Langford. I was falling in love with Frances Langford.

Chapter 2
Frances Langford

Frances was discovered by Rudy Vallee in the early 1930s, so I guess you could say I "re"-discovered her in 2006. The song she will forever be associated and remembered for is the wonderful "I'm in the Mood for Love," which was written especially for her by the popular song writing team of Dorothy Fields and Jimmy McHugh and featured in her first movie, 1935's *Every Night at Eight*. This movie starred Frances, Alice Faye, and Patsy Kelly . . . and George Raft playing a band leader!

In 1936 at the age of 23, Frances made a movie for Paramount entitled *Palm Springs*. In it she featured a lovely ballad called "Will I Ever Know." Playing a young carefree heiress with a boatload of suitors and not finding any of them "suitable," she muses over her situation, singing. As she sings the words, "The moment that I see him I will know him, no matter how impossible it seems. I know just what he'll do, I know just what he'll say, we have met before in dreams." That was it! I knew she was singing about me! And I knew that she was what I had been searching for. Dreaming for.

"Cut!" said director Aubrey Scotto jubilantly. "Print! Frances, that was simply wonderful!"

"What................. Oh yes, uh, thank you," said Frances. "Take fifteen, everybody," yelled Scotto.

"Honey, you were really terrif," said Iris Adrian, coming onto the set which depicted

Will I Ever Know

Frances in her bedroom. It was 1936 and they were filming the movie *Palm Springs*.

"How many takes to do the song?"

"Just one," said Frances, "just one."

"What's the matter, dearie, you look like you're a million miles away."

"It's that song, Iris, every time I sing it, I expect something to happen." "Like?" asked Iris.

"I don't know," said Frances. "I guess I expect Prince Charming to suddenly appear and take me away."

"That decanter over there must be filled with something more than just tea," quipped Iris.

"But Iris, the question, 'Will I Ever Know.' I want to experience what the song says. I want to meet someone like that, someone I've known forever but don't know."

"Honey, you got me all confused. I wouldn't say that to too many people, the guys in the white coats will whisk you away."

"But I've been dreaming about a man," she continued. "I can't quite see his face, he comes just so close and then fades away."

"Listen, you get ol' Smith Ballew to teach you how to use that rope. Next time you're dreamin', lasso that 'dream' man with it. Maybe you can brand him too."

Frances laughed. "Oh you, I bet that's just what you'd do too. I'm afraid a rope wouldn't work for my phantom. I just can't get 'him' out of my mind."

"Fran, you're working too hard, you're excited about this picture, and don't forget, you're a newlywed, your Prince Charming is waiting for you at.........well, on the set of his movie."

"Jon's nice enough, and I really love him, I suppose, but this . . .this is something differ-ent."

Charles Henry

I might interject here that Smith Ballew was Frances' co-star in the movie *Palm Springs*. He was a handsome western star and actually the first "singing" cowboy in films. And Frances had just married Jon Hall, a rugged athletic actor who became famous for his adventure movies.

"Listen, Iris," said Frances. "I have to go back to my dressing room, we're on a 15 minute break, we'll talk there."

"I gotta better idea," said Iris. "Meet me for lunch, come over to the set when you're free. We're just doing a read-through so I can go anytime."

"Okay," said Frances. "I'll see you there."

Chapter 3
Obsession

As my obsession grew, I had this burning desire to meet Frances Langford, to tell her how wonderful she is, to tell her about the effect on me of "Will I Ever Know," but there were two things that made this very difficult.

1) She died in 2005.
2) If she were alive, she would be 94 years old.

Dating older women is one thing but..............................34 and 94—well, that's a little much. I began to dream of time travel. Going back in time, meeting and wooing this intoxicating woman. "Oh Chad, you foolish dreamer," I said to myself on many occasions. "Get your head out of the clouds and concentrate on the things you need to do like GET A JOB, find a girl, a real girl. Get real!"

My parents were saying the same thing. Someone has said, "The reality is never as good as the fantasy." Yeah right. Of course, I never listen to myself. And so it continued, Frances in the car singing, Frances at home on the TV screen, singing, Frances on the computer, me searching always for more information, more photos, more music. Frances in my dreams, in my arms, in my heart. "NO MATTER HOW IMPOSSIBLE IT SEEMS."

My father suggested I get a job at the post office. That didn't really appeal to me. My mother suggested I go to school for computer programming. Reluctantly, I enrolled in one of those "technical schools," but after about three weeks I dropped out. I really didn't know which way was up and after fouling up the school's computer with a "test" program, they weren't sorry to see me go.

They're probably still trying to unravel what I had done.

Chapter 4
The Job

One day, while perusing the want ads, an item jumped out at me: "WANTED: ASSOCIATE TO WORK ON TIME MACHINE, low pay, long hours, fascinating position. Contact: Prof. Ernst Von Schlaben 215-555-5555." Was I dreaming? I read and re-read the ad. This seemed like an answer to my prayers! Going back, say to 1945 to meet Frances. But was this professor legitimate? Or was this some kind of gag? Well, it wouldn't hurt to find out. I called the number and a very heavily accented German voice answered the phone. "Yah, vat can I do for you?"

"Is this Prof. Von Schlaban?" I asked. "Ja, this is Herr Von Schlaban, who is dis?"

"I'm Chad Henson, I'm calling about your ad in the paper for an assistant, I'm very interested in the position."

"Ja Ja, okay, let me tell you, the chob vill be to organize, catergorize, familiarize yourself with all of my notes, plans, prototypes, schematics, etc., etc., and be able to locate them ven I need them. There is absolutely no order here, ach du lieber. Ven can you start?"

It sounded like I had the job. I was getting excited. "Right away, sir," I said.

I made arrangements to go right over to his place. As I left my apartment, I was trying to figure out how I could con the professor into thinking I knew something about math and physics. I'd do anything to ride that Time Machine back to 1945. Clutching my scrap-

Charles Henry

book of Frances memorabilia, off I went.

The professor lived on the outskirts of Center City, Elm Street. It was a once-fashionable neighborhood that had fallen on hard times but was coming back.

As I came upon the professor's Victorian brownstone, I noticed that most of the homes on his street seemed like they had been converted into apartments, lofts, etc. But the prof's home looked like it was still a single family dwelling. I anxiously knocked at the door and was met by a wild-eyed man about 70 years old with Einstein-like hair, moustache, and goatee.

As I stood in the main hall, I could see to my left a study, to the right a large living room, and straight ahead a large circular staircase with the dining room and kitchen behind.

"Mr. Henson, come in, I am Ernst Von Schlaban, my lab is on the third floor," declared the professor. "Come, ve talk."

After climbing what seemed like forever, we came upon the third-floor lab. There was all sorts of clutter. Paper, paper everywhere, prototypes of inventions, notes, drawings, everything in no order at all. The clutter spilled into the other two rooms on that floor.

"Young man," said the professor, "your chob, as I said on the phone, vill be to organize, put in order, and file all of this." He made a large sweeping gesture to let me know that I was to work in all three rooms.
"And your pay vill be $300 a veek, dats all I can afford." This seemed like a lifelong task, but since the professor was willing to pay me $300 a week and considering my current financial status, it made me feel like a rich man. However, that wasn't my real purpose in being there. I agreed to take the job.

The professor said, "Vould you like to see the Time Machine?" "Yes, of course!" was my excited cry.

Chapter 5
The Professor

Prof. Ernst Von Schlaban was a rather well-known teacher and scholar in physics. He had studied under the noted Dr. Wolfgang Gertl in Munich and later became his assistant. In turn, Dr. Gertl was a pupil of Dr. Walter Wolf, who in turn had done experimental work on the space-time continuum with Betelmann and Guenther. It was Dr. Gertl who pioneered the multi-dimensional theory, which states that there are actually innumerable dimensions which we are not aware of, in which everything that ever happened continues to happen simultaneously. It was his dream to be able to break into these dimensions with time travel, so theoretically one could go from one year to the other, one century to the other.

Where Gertl split with Wolf was on whether you could change something that happened in the past. Wolf's position was no, once something happened in the past it stayed that way. No time traveler could undo anything that was done in the past. Gertl took the position that you COULD change the past by doing time traveling, and that you had better be very careful in your time travel because something that you might change could alter events all through history with the potential of turning the COSMOS INTO CHAOS. Altering just one small thing could have a domino effect that would ultimately destroy the universe. That was Von Schlaban's position also.

After Dr. Gertl's death in 1984, Prof. Von Schlaban emigrated to the U.S. and landed in Philadelphia and got a teaching position at the University of Pennsylvania, working on the Time Machine in his spare time.

Charles Henry

I asked Prof. Von Schlaban why he didn't get one of his students, or someone from the university, someone with a background in physics, to assist him.

The professor said, "I don't vant to do that. The academic world can be brutal. Someone with a little knowledge could steal my ideas, my plans, with access to my notes and vork, they could be sold to the highest bidder and who knows whose hands they vould fall into? I prefer someone with no knowledge of anything." He had described me perfectly.

All of this sounded like some sci-fi fantasy to me, yet the $300 a week and the possibility of going back in time to meet Frances was enticing. But oh, the mess! The professor wanted me to start right away.

I got right to work. I figured the first step was to try to organize everything by year, then go from there. "Oh," said the professor, "you wanted to see the machine, come, this vay." We went into the room containing the machine.

Chapter 6
The Time Machine

And there it was: a computer, a control panel with all sorts of keys other than the typewriting keyboard, and to the right was what looked like an old-fashioned telephone booth which was the transporter. I went over and peeked inside the transporter. It was empty—no buttons, no phone, no nothing.

The professor pointed out each part of the machine and said, "Once you get into the transporter and I hit the SEND button, within seconds you are in your destination. Unfortunately there is not a RETURN button as of yet. That is vat I am vorking on now. If you find anything that says 'reverse' or 'reverse-a-tron' gear, hold them out and give them to me immediately. Dis is vat is holding up the whole thing. I can't get dis damn gear to vork."

The professor then said, "Anyvay, hypothetically speaking, if someday you could go back in time, do you have a year, person, place that you might like to wisit?"

Without hesitation, I told the professor of my obsession with Frances Langford and that I wanted to go back to Sept. 17, 1945, RKO studios, 11:15 a.m. Pacific Time.

"Ah, Frances Langford," exclaimed the professor, "a real cutie, vun of my favorites."

I showed the professor my scrapbook of Frances memorabilia. "My, you've got quite an assortment of items there, it must have taken years for you to accumulate all of that."

Charles Henry

"No, not really," I said. "With the computer, it's only taken a little over a year."

"Ach du lieber," said the professor. "Vat an age ve live in."

I didn't tell the professor about "Will I Ever Know." I didn't want him to think I was as crazy as he was.

The professor typed in "FRANCES LANGFORD," and immediately her life history popped up on the screen, year by year. 1913-2005. The professor told me that I could now visit any year that she was alive.

"I'm ready to go now," I said to the professor as I eagerly stepped into the booth. "Ah, not so fast, young man, there is a slight problem. As I said, I can send you, that is no problem. Bringing you back is the problem. I haven't figured out how to do that yet."

"I don't care," I said. "I don't really want to come back once I find Frances." "Oh, but you must come back," said the professor. "Who knows what you might accidentally do? Wisits back in time must be short and with a definite purpose, mostly research. Time travel is not for play. You must promise that you won't change anything because it could set off that domino effect and cause the cosmos to become chaos."

"Okay," I said, "I won't spill the beans on what's going to happen. I promise. Can I go back now to 1945?"

"No no no," said the professor. "Don't you understand? I just told you, it's not ready, I sent a dog and two cats back to 1860 two months ago and I can't bring them back. Ve need more testing."

Testing schmesting, thought I. I wanted to get to see Frances on the set of *The Bamboo Blond*, which I knew was in production at that time.

"Come, enough of this, ve vill see if you vill be the one to test the finished product, but for now, ve must get to vork," said the professor.

My first day with Prof. Von Schlaban was a rather long one. I had gotten to his home around 11 a.m. and I didn't leave till half past eight. He said he wanted me to report by 8 a.m., and stay till whenever; so much for keeping my delicate balance between sloth and inactivity. Ah, what you won't do for love!

Chapter 7
Advice From A Friend

I had just about gotten home when the phone rang. It was my friend from high school, Larry Savage. Larry had taken another route than I had after high school. He went to Drexel University and ended up with a job as an adjunct to the city controller. Nobody actually knows what that is, including Larry, but he goes to work every day and brings home a nice paycheck every week. I asked him on several occasions about getting me a job in city hall. The only response I would get was, "I'm looking into it, Chad, I'm looking into it." He has a nice small office in city hall with a large desk that has absolutely nothing on it except a very expensive-looking pen set.

Larry is married with three kids—slightly more than the national average of 2.5 children, two girls and a boy.

Larry's job requires him to live in the city so he and his wife, Gloria, found a house as close to the suburbs as they could get. In fact, the suburbs are literally right across the street. They are almost right on the city line.

"Hey, Chad," said Larry. "What's new?"

"Great news, Lar," I said. "I started a job today with some professor from the University of Pennsylvania, out on west Elm Street. I'm his 'assistant,' no less."

Charles Henry

"Well, congrats, ol' boy, what will you be doing?"

"I guess I'm sort of a file clerk/maintenance man. I'm organizing 40 years of notes, etc. It should only take me 50 years to do it."

"Maybe you'll be motivated to take some courses then," said Larry.

"He's a physics professor, I doubt that I'm going to be 'motivated' by any of that, but he is working on a Time Machine. I'm looking forward to having him send me back in time to meet Frances."

Larry was all too familiar with my passion for "La Langford," as he called her. I had exposed him to Frances; he was mildly interested but his musical tastes were centered on countless Heavy Metal groups, which was okay, but Larry's head was definitely in the present.

"Listen, Mac," he said, "sounds crazy to me, better watch this old guy. Some of those old profs get a little wifty. I wouldn't count on taking any time travels very soon. But at least you have a job. Now we have to get you a girl. Admit it, 'La Langford' is gone, history, belongs to the ages. Concentrate on someone in the here and now. There's a new girl on our floor at work, Heather, Heavenly Heather"—he chuckled—"cute as a button and really built. I'll find out what her situation is and let you know."

"You do that, Larry, old friend, I'll take my chances with Frances in 1945."

"You're crazy," said Larry. "Invite me to the wedding."

"You'll be my best man, Lar."

"I better reserve a tux" was his sarcastic reply. "I gotta go, Gloria has me doing the wash, she's out at a PTA meeting."

How exciting, I thought. "Okay, Mr. Mom, get to your chores." And we hung up.

Chapter 8
Working With The Professor

The professor turned out to be a rather stern taskmaster but fun at the same time. He would take long breaks and tell me stories of his exploits in Germany, how he and Dr. Gertl had had a Time Machine almost ready for testing in 1977, but then there was a fire in their lab and the machine was completely destroyed along with their notes and schematics.

The fire was of a suspicious origin, the professors alleging that it was the work of a rival colleague who was jealous of their impending success. Nothing ever came of it.

After almost three weeks of work, I was getting nowhere fast with my "organizing," and I was getting very antsy about making the trip back to 1945.

I asked Von Schlaban on several occasions if he'd let me test the Time Machine by going back to 1945, and I got his standard, stock answer: "It's not ready yet, I let you know ven. It's that Reverse-a-tron gear." Needless to say in my organizing and filing, I was keeping a lookout for anything that said "reverse" or "reverse-a-tron." I found some pages with "reverse-a-tron" on them but they were "32 of 511" or "236 of 511," not much in between, and not the pages he was especially looking for.

I spent my spare time listening to Frances' records and watching her movies. I bought mp3 discs of old radio shows, wading through hours of material just to hear Frances do one song. I had to meet her. I had to see her. I had to go back in time!

Charles Henry

Then one day an opportunity presented itself. I was in the Time Machine room with the professor. He usually never left me in there alone.

"Ach du lieber," cried the professor, "I can't find page 318 of the plans for that damn reverse-a-tron gear. There are still so many pages missing. I vas just looking at it, I know I had it. Maybe I left it somevere on the second floor. I be right back, keep vorking."

A handful of dusty files in my hands, the idea hit me! Now was my chance. He had programmed everything that was needed; all I needed to do was push the SEND button and hop into the booth.

Chapter 9
Off I Go

I hesitantly typed "FRANCES LANGFORD" on the subject line. Immediately all of her biographical data popped up on the screen. I typed in the date, time, and location of the destination, SEPTEMBER 17, 1945 11:15 A.M., RKO STUDIOS, HOLLYWOOD, CALIFORNIA. A new screen popped up with all the information and one other word . . . SEND. I had no idea how long the professor would be gone looking for his missing page. This was it. Now or never!

I pushed the SEND button and quickly jumped into the transporter booth, closing the door and clutching my book of memorabilia. I was taking it to prove to Frances that I really was from the future. There were many post-1945 photos in the scrapbook.

The machine sprang to life. My senses were bombarded by flashing lights and gurgling sounds like some kind of boiling liquid; in other words, I felt like I was in some weird '50s science-fiction movie. Then I felt myself fading away as the room began to get fainter and fainter. I was GOOOOOOOOOOOOOOOOOOOING. . .

Meanwhile, the professor, hearing all the sounds from the third floor, knew what I had done.

"Ach du lieber!" shouted the professor as he ran over to the control panel and in his angst, began pushing all sorts of buttons at random, trying to cancel the command like mad. "I've got to get him back!" cried the professor.

Part II
1995

Chapter 10
I Arrive . . . In Jensen Beach, FL?

All of a sudden I was in a tumbling motion and plopped down rather unceremoniously on a well-manicured lawn.

I looked up and saw a beautiful inn/restaurant. I didn't know where I was or what year it was. From the looks of the cars in the parking lot, it looked like the mid-'90s. The professor had obviously realized what I'd done and was messing around with the controls.

The sign on the front of the complex read "DOLPHIN BAR and SHRIMP HOUSE." That name seemed familiar somehow to me. That's right! It was the former "OUTRIGGER" restaurant that Frances and her second husband, Ralph Evinrude, owned up until his death in 1986. Frances sold the restaurant, but she remained a welcome frequent patron.

I walked into the restaurant, and, glancing at a newspaper at the desk, I saw it was Sept 17, 1995! I knew that even though she no longer owned the restaurant, she still spent a lot of time there, interacting with the guests and occasionally singing some of her songs. I was glad that the attire was casual so I didn't look too out of place in my T-shirt and jeans, although I wished I had dressed up a bit.

I did a quick look see through the restaurant and. . . there she was! She was sitting at a large table with some guests. I walked up to the desk of the Maitre d' to request a table. The name on the engraved plate on the front of the desk read Carter Halsey Maitre d'."

Charles Henry

The Maitre d' was busily engaged in a conversation with one of the waiters.

"But I told you about the Fineman party of twelve yesterday, that table should be set and 'RESERVED,' they will be here any minute."

"No, this is the first I've heard of it," replied the waiter. "Now the configuration of the room will be out of kilter. I'm going to have to squeeze them in at station 14."

"My good fellow," stated Halsey, "You don't 'squeeze' in the Finemans, you seat them prominently in station 4 or station 5. Maxine is their favorite server, anyone else is unacceptable."

The waiter, Thompson, replied, very annoyed, "Maxine's station is full, she can't handle any more, let alone a party of twelve."

"Handle them she will, Thompson, handle them she will, and room will be made for them," said Halsey.

As Thompson continued his protest, I made a beeline past them and headed right for Frances. She looked like she was in her 80s but still sharp as a tack, still with that winning smile.

Chapter 11
Frances Langford At 82

"Miss Langford," I stammered, "excuse me but I've come a long way to see you." Our eyes met, and she said quizzically, "Do I know you? You look rather familiar."

"Well, we haven't actually met before, except in dreams." Frances jumped as I said that. "What's wrong?" I asked her. "Are you alright?"

"Oh yes," she replied, "its just that as you said that an old song of mine was going through my head, 'Will I Ever Know'."

Excited I exclaimed, "*Palm Springs*, 1936, Paramount." "Why yes," she said, pleased and with an absolutely sweet smile on her face. "That song has haunted me for years."

I looked at her intensely and quoted the lines from the song: "The moment that I see him I will know him, no matter how impossible it seems, I know just what he'll do, I know just what he'll say, we have met before in dreams."

Frances did indeed recognize me, albeit faintly. She was having what Professor Von Schlaban would later explain to me as a "past memory of future events." Because he had tinkered with the year that I wanted to return to, Frances was remembering events of the past, which had not happened yet. That's why it was a very faint memory.

What wasn't faint was the effect that the song "Will I Ever Know" had on her. She was clearly moved and touched by it and this made me very happy, as I knew it was bringing us together. I knew she was associating it with me.

We stared at each other for a time, then Frances said, as if awaking from a reverie, "This is my husband, Harold," as she tapped him on the shoulder and I shook hands with Frances' third husband, Harold Stuart.

"Pleased to meet you, young man," he said as he rose with outstretched hand. "Likewise," I said. "My name is Chad Henson and I'm a big fan of your wife." Immediately after I said that, I felt stupid and awkward but Harold put me at ease by saying, "So am I." "I didn't realize I had any fans under 80," joked Frances. We all laughed.

"Please join us," said Frances. "Pull up a chair. I'll have Maxine set you a place." She called Maxine over and informed her that I was joining them.

There were two other couples at the table. After introductions were made, I said to Frances, "I have so much of your music on CDs and albums, and I love your movies, I'm getting a lot of them on tape."

"I'm glad somebody likes my movies," said Frances. "I thought I was the only one who did." We all laughed again.

Looking at my memorabilia book, Frances asked, "What is this?"

"Oh," I replied, "its my scrapbook of you, photos, movie posters, etc. Could I have you sign some of them?"

"I'll sign them all," Frances replied enthusiastically. "Harold, may I borrow your pen?"

Harold took a pen out of his shirt pocket and gave it to Frances. As she worked away she said, "I'm not only signing them, I'm dating them, that way you'll remember exactly when they were signed. Sept 17, 1995."
The book being rather thick, this signing process was going to take some time.

The small band was playing "I'm in the Mood for Love," and the people in the restaurant were begging Frances to join in. She stopped her signing, put the pen down, and joined the band. She sang the last chorus, and at 82 her voice still held the same passion and sultry tone it always had. My heart leaped as the audience showered her with applause and bravos.

As the excitement died down, I gushed, "Oh, Frances, that was sublime!"

"You're very kind," she said. "I'm glad they picked a song I'm slightly familiar with!" That got a big rise out of everybody at the table.

"Where are you staying?" she asked.

I replied, "I'm not actually staying anywhere, I just sort of 'dropped' in." I was wiping at the grass stains on my pants and shirt.

"You must stay with us up at the big house," Frances exclaimed. "I won't take 'no' for an answer. Do you like fishing?" she asked.

"Oh, I love it!" I cried. "Although it's been a long time since I've done any."

"We're going out tomorrow, I insist you come with us. We'll outfit you completely," said Frances with a smile.

Frances and Harold treated me to a wonderful dinner, some sort of Polynesian dish that I couldn't pronounce, let alone spell. After dinner and coffee, we three walked up to their home.

Their home was a lovely "split-level" affair with a sunken living room. The living room was filled with celebrity pictures, all autographed to Frances. "Say, fella," said Frances, "you've got a ton of stuff in this scrapbook, I'll leave it in your room when I'm done signing." We settled in for some decaf coffee and some Bundt cake.

I was given a room next to Frances and her husband, Harold, an amiable sort of chap, very pleasant and highly energetic. He seemed a good match for the 82-year-old Frances.

I still couldn't believe that I was there in 1995, although this was not the way I had planned it. The professor had to have tinkered with the settings because I knew the machine was programmed for 1945, not 1995.

Charles Henry

I fell into a fitful sleep dreaming of the 1945 Frances running to me but never quite getting there and us calling to each other over the deep chasm of time and space.

I awoke with a start at 5 a.m. I saw that the scrapbook had been placed on my night table. I thumbed through it and Frances had signed and dated every item. Bless her heart, I thought. I think I'm falling in love with the 82-year-old Frances. This is crazy, but the song lyrics came back to my memory: "No matter how impossible it seems." I wasn't going to fight it. I wasn't going to complain because here I was with Frances, who after all was really the same Frances as in 1945, just 50 years older! She was the same glorious singer and personality that she'd always been.

Chapter 12
Fishing With Frances & Harold

Breakfast was in the grand dining room overlooking a gorgeous lake. Frances looked radiant even in her fishing gear. Hal came in all ready for the fishing expedition. My "borrowed" fishing outfit was a little tight on me, but I was sure the fish wouldn't mind and neither would Frances.

We made small talk over the meal. Hal asked me some questions about myself. I tried to answer in a way that I wouldn't betray my knowledge of the future.

I diverted the talk of me to questions about Frances and her career. What was her favorite song? Which movie was her favorite of all the ones she'd made? What did she think of the current music as opposed to the sounds of the '30s and '40s? What is Bob Hope really like?

This kept the conversation going and Frances seemed happy to wax nostalgic about her glorious past. Hal seemed to enjoy her reminiscences as much as I did. I could see how devoted he was to her.

After breakfast it was time to board the *Chanticleer*. This was not your typical fishing boat. It was a yacht, fully staffed with all the amenities of a floating home. I found out that this was not just a day trip, but that we would be out for three days. I didn't mind, I wasn't going anywhere . . . or was I? The sky was blue, the breezes light and refreshing. The water was calm.

Charles Henry

We were just going to sail up and down the river for three days, fishing and relaxing. While we had our lines in the water, Frances started asking questions about me. I decided to tell her the truth that I was from the future. What could she do besides call the men in the white coats?

I told her everything, from the professor through the Time Machine travel. She didn't flinch. She didn't say a word but she began humming, "Will I Ever Know." She looked at me and said, "I believe you, Chad, I don't know why but I believe you are from the future, maybe I'm just a crazy old woman."

I looked over at Hal. He had fallen asleep. Frances told me how that song had stayed with her all these years.

"I've had three husbands and got to know millions of servicemen," she laughed, "but never found the man in the song, until. . ." Hal woke up with a start as his fishing line snapped alive with a catch. We both watched him reel in a good-size fish. I was waiting for Frances to finish that sentence. She never did but somehow I knew what she would have said and strange as it seems, I was very happy.

Chapter 13
At The Movies

That evening, after dinner, we went into the lounge of the ship. It was set up like a small movie theater, complete with theater seats. A large screen was set up in the front with a very old but very expensive-looking projector in the back.

"I thought we might watch a movie tonight," said Frances. "I had Harold load up *The Bamboo Blond*, I hope that's okay with you."

"My absolute favorite," I said. "It will be great to see it on a big screen." "This was supposed to be my 'break through' film," said Frances, "but it didn't happen."

"I can't understand it," I said. "You are absolutely wonderful in it, everybody was really terrific in it and the songs are really good too."

"Well, Chad, Hollywood can be a fun place but it can also be very cruel. If you're not part of the 'in crowd' and play the politics, it can be very rough. Just like in any industry."

I thought of the "politics" at Value Barn and I knew what she meant.

"Maybe if I hadn't been away so much, you know, touring, entertaining the troops, things may have been different, but I wouldn't change anything. Being with those brave boys and seeing the smiles on their faces, bringing them a little bit of 'home,' that's what I was all about. All of that is worth everything to me. It's the most satisfying part of my career."

Hal piped up, "we couldn't have won the war without you, dear, and I mean that."

"Oh, Hal, you're so sweet, it's flattering to think that I had even a small part in keeping morale up."

"Listen," said Hal, "I was very involved with the troops during the war and afterward in the Truman administration, and I heard your praises sung from the top military echelons down to the PFCs. They all loved you and adored you." Frances looked embarrassed but very pleased. You could tell she had no regrets.

"One thing about working in 'B' films…"—I started to protest the "B" films comment but Frances held up her hand to stop me—"Working in 'B' films," she continued, "you didn't have to deal with 'super inflated ego's,' temper tantrums, 'star' demands. Oh, there were some little skirmishes, once in awhile you'd get someone who was really taken with themselves, but for the most part we were an ensemble. Everyone working hard together, that's the important word, together, to do their very best in a short amount of time. The studios had us on a tight schedule. A month of shooting was a luxury. They didn't pour a lot of money into those movies so there were no gorgeous sets or costumes to divert the public's attention. It was up to us. Everyone pulling together, and I think when you see these movies today, they play really well, very tight, very creative, and rank right up there with our more 'expensive' cousins, the 'A' films."

"I couldn't agree with you more, Frances, I love the 'B' movies and I really admire the actors who populated them," I said.

"Hey, let's not forget about our movie," said Frances. "Roll 'em, Harold." And we all had a good laugh.

As Harold started the movie, I couldn't believe I was watching this movie with the star herself. "There's Ralph Edwards," said Frances. "What a nice man, and most people forget what an excellent actor and comedian he was. More than just the 'game show' guy. So wonderful to work with."

As the movie continued, Frances would punctuate the action with some reminiscences about what was going on. I wish I could have taped her comments.

Will I Ever Know

The plot of *The Bamboo Blond* is really cute. A flyer is mistakenly told to meet his buddies in a nightclub that, unknown to him, is off-limits to servicemen.

Frances is the singer at the club. She befriends the flyboy and finds out it's his last night at home before shipping out.

Iris Adrian plays her sidekick as she did in a couple of other movies. Frances treats him to a meal at a local mom-and-pop eatery. They dance, Frances sings, and you can see there is some real chemistry going on there.

Frances thinks he's a poor farm boy, but in reality he is the son of a wealthy farm owner in Bucks County, Pa. She sees him off at the airport and he has her picture taken in one of those 25¢ photo booths. He is going to carry it with him for luck. His buddies arrive as they share a long goodbye kiss. They razz him about the "beautiful blond," she rushes off, and he doesn't even know her name!

For good luck one of the crew paints Frances' picture on the front of their plane using the small photo booth picture as a model. Since no one knows her name, they dub the plane "The Bamboo Blond," the color of Frances' hair. This brings them good luck and a trip back to the states to do a war bond drive. In the end, Frances and the flier get together and live happily ever after.

After the movie ended, Frances said, "How about another one, Chad? My movies are short." We all laughed.

"Okay, sure, what else do you have onboard?" "*Radio Stars on Parade*, from 1945," she said. "Great, I love that movie too." Hal loaded up the projector once again and started it rolling.

Radio Stars on Parade stars Frances in a familiar role, the aspiring singer looking to break into the big-time world of show business, has some wonderful music, and features Frances at the end of the movie singing "That Ol' Black Magic."

"I loved making that movie," said Frances. "All of those zany people, it was great fun."

Chapter 14
Off Again

The next morning after breakfast, Frances and I went out on the deck to watch the morning develop. Hal stayed below to do the dishes.

"I wish you could stay with us forever," said Frances with a dreamy look in her eye. "So do I," I replied, "but I have no idea how long I'm going to stay anywhere."

"I'll speak to them at the restaurant, maybe we can get you a job there."

"That would be great, Frances, I think I'm going to like it here."

"How many fish you gonna catch today, Chad?" asked Frances. "Twice as many as yesterday," I replied, "and since I caught zero yesterday, I guess that means a double zero." Frances laughed that melodic laugh of hers.

We both cast our lines into the water. Harold came up on deck and put his line in. "Not much action," I said. "The fish must know there's a stranger in their midst." "Funny," said Frances. "I feel as if I've known you forever, Chad."

"Frances, I feel the same way, definitely, maybe for me it's the result of watching your movies, and 'Will I Ever Know'."

Frances had that look in her eye again. "It's the same and more for me, that crazy song keeps going through my head."

We looked at each other for a long time and we knew.

Meanwhile back at the lab, Prof. Von Schlaban was knee-deep in plans and notes trying to get me back. "Ah, this should do it," said the professor. "Vun little push of the button"

I squeezed Frances' hand and thanked her for wanting me to stay. I leaned over to give her a little kiss, when all of a sudden I could feel myself slipping, as if I were being pulled away from the deck. The boat seemed so far away. I yelled, "Frances!!!!!!!!" I was fading out, getting fainter and fainter. .... "Chad!!!!!!" screamed Frances, "no, no, come back," as she gave way to hysterical tears.

Part III
1945

Chapter 15
September 17, 1945

I was floating again between the earth and the heavens. After what seemed like forever I landed, knocking two people over. As I regained my bearings, one of the persons that I bowled over was none other than Frances! But she was so much younger! Now I recognized where I was; I was on the set of the movie *The Bamboo Blond*. The "MOM'S PANTRY" set. I was back to 1945! Russell Wade, her co-star in the movie, and I helped her to her feet.

"Where did you come from?" she asked quizzically but good naturedly. The contents of my memorabilia notebook were scattered all over the floor. I must have had it in my hand on deck of the *Chanticleer* when I got zapped, although I don't remember having it with me.

"What's the meaning of this?" came the voice of Russell Wade. Now the director, Anthony Mann, was there, having a fit because the scene was ruined.

"What's going on here? Who is this guy and why is he here, right in the middle of the scene? We're on a tight schedule, you know."

"It's all right, Tony, I'll take care of it," said Frances.

"I'm terribly sorry," I stammered, "are you alright? I mean you no harm, I'm a big fan, I've come such a long way to see you, Miss Langford."

Charles Henry

Frances began helping me pick up all of my memorabilia. She looked into my eyes and said quizzically, "Say, do I know you, stranger? You look sort of familiar." Frances was having what Professor Von Schlaben would call a "future memory," having met her in 1995. In her 1945 world that was in the future, but still it happened so she was actually recalling something from the future.

"That's a long story," I said, hoping I didn't sound too mysterious.

"Would you like me to autograph some of these items?" asked Frances. "Uh, well, that is............" I stammered. Before I could finish, Frances said, "Why, they're all autographed by me and dated 1995, that's 50 years from now." We gazed intently into each other's eyes and I knew she knew. "The moment that I see him I will know him."

Chapter 16
Trying To Explain

"Uh, well, Miss Langford, I told you I had come a long way to see you."

"Well, now I'm really confused," said Frances. "Come back to my dressing room and explain it to me slooooooowly," she said with a twinkle in her eye. "Tony," said Frances, "why don't we break for lunch?"

"Alright," he said, "everything's ruined anyway. Lunch everybody. Then we'll redo the whole scene, including the song."

As he walked away, he shouted, "One hour, and can anybody tell me who the hell this guy is?"

"You want me to go with you?" asked Russell.

"That's okay," replied Frances. "Uh………….." "Chad," I chirped in. "Yes," said Frances, "Chad's an old friend who just 'dropped' in unexpectedly, he's going to show me his scrapbook."

"Dropped in," said Russell sarcastically. "Damn near killed both of us."

He went off to join Tony Mann, who was having a mild rant at losing this important scene. It had gone very well up to the time that I burst in.

"Don't worry about Tony," said Frances. "His bark is worse than his bite. We're at least three days ahead of schedule anyway. And Russell gets upset when more than three strands of his hair get mussed."

"That's a relief, I'm really sorry about ruining the scene."

"That's okay, I wasn't really satisfied with it anyway. We would probably have redone it eventually."

So off to her dressing room we went. Frances didn't say any more as we walked in silence. This is your big chance, Chad, I said to myself. Don't blow it; you've got to convince her who you are and why you are here.

We got to her dressing room and it was just what you would expect from Frances. Warm pastel colors, flowered wallpaper, a large dressing table with all sorts of make-up, perfumes, etc., two large Queen Anne chairs, and a large sofa. She pulled me to the sofa and we sat down.

"Now, Chad, uh…………………." "Henson," I stammered, "Chad Henson."

"Now, Chad Henson," she continued, "just what is going on here?"

Sitting that close to Frances, her long blond hair taking on a halo-like glow, that marvelous figure, that beautiful face, I wasn't sure of anything at the moment. All I wanted to do was swim in those beautiful brown eyes.

I had no other choice but to blurt out the whole story—about losing my job, the divorce, discovering Frances on a new type of record called a "CD," listening to "Will I Ever Know," haunted by the words.

At the mention of "Will I Ever Know," she stiffened and clenched her fists. I had hit a nerve. I continued telling her about answering Prof. Von Schlaban's ad to work on the Time Machine just so I could get back to meet her, only to find out the professor just wanted a lackey to clean up and organize his considerable mess.

I told her how he'd programmed the machine for 1945, *The Bamboo Blond* set, but that he wouldn't send me because he didn't know how to bring me back. And that once he'd left the room, I sent myself into time, and that he must have tinkered with it in some way,

Will I Ever Know

because I landed in 1995, not 1945, but now I'm here. Phew! Listening to the stumbling, bumbling way I explained it, I didn't really believe it myself.

Frances looked skeptical. I couldn't tell from her face whether I was Prince Charming or a lunatic on the run. "Wow, soldier," she said, "that's a lot to chew on."

Suddenly she gave a start and looked dreamily away. "Miss Langford, are you alright?"

"Chad, my name is Frances, no more of this Miss Langford stuff. That old song just crept into my head, 'Will I Ever Know'." I started singing "The moment that I see him I will know him, no matter how impossible it seems." She took over, singing "I know just what he'll do, I know just what he'll say, we have met before in dreams."

"Frances," I said, "when I first heard that song I knew I had to meet you, I knew it was meant for me."

"Chad," said Frances, "I want to believe you but do I dare? Time travel, that's the stuff that science fiction is made of."

I said, "I know, it kind of scares me too. But look at my scrapbook, you admitted that was your handwriting and signature."

"I know," said Frances, "but put yourself in my shoes. A man comes hurtling onto the movie set, tells me he is from the future, and shows me all those pictures and clippings that I supposedly signed fifty years from now, it's all so bizarre."

"Look, Frances, there are pictures here from the '50s, '60s, '70s, '80s, '90s." She didn't say a word. "Let me show you the money of the future." I pulled out a wad of the new tens and twenties, and also the new coins. "Oh, and here's my driver's license, picture and everything, in plastic." Again, Frances looked both puzzled and skeptical.

"Wait a minute," said Frances. "I'll be right back." I sat there feeling rather dejected. It seemed like it was easier to convince the 1995 Frances who I was.

Chapter 17
An Invitation

Iris Adrian was having a flirty conversation with Russell Wade. Frances rushed over and pulled her away.

"Excuse us, Russ," said Frances. "I've got to talk to Iris, it's important." "No problem, ladies, I'll see you both on the set after lunch." And he walked over to where Tony Mann and some others were standing.

"What's the matter with you, Fran? I was scoring some points with Capt. Cutie there."

"Iris, there's someone here I want you to meet. Says his name is Chad Henson and that he's from the year 2007 and time traveled back here just to meet me."

"Well, now I've heard it all," said Iris. "I'll call the police and have this nut removed!"

"You'll do no such thing, Miss Adrian," said Frances. "Remember when I sang that song 'Will I Ever Know' for the *Palm Springs* movie? Well, I think I've found my phantom man. I looked deep in his eyes and I knew, I really knew!"

"Oh brother," said Iris, "I smell a con game here."

"Never mind that, I've never felt like this, it's like the search is over. I'm happy, excited, and peaceful all at the same time. I'm going to invite him to stay at the house for a couple of days and you're coming too, we'll find out if he's legit or I'm crazy."

Frances was back in a few minutes. I breathed a sigh of relief when I saw her; I wasn't sure if she was coming back or calling the police.

"Chad, I want you to meet my dear friend Iris Adrian. Iris, this is Chad Henson."

"Pleased to make your acquaintance I'm sure," said Iris with a REAL skeptical look on her face. "I love your movies, Iris," I said. "Uh-huh" was Iris's lackluster response.

"Chad," said Frances, "I need to know more about this. Why don't you come stay at my house in Palm Springs for a few days, Jon is away on location and I've invited Iris to come too." I was busting but I didn't want to look too pleased. I knew that Iris Adrian was coming along as a "chaperone," and that I was being put on a sort of probation.

"Fine with me, Frances," I said. "When do we leave?" "Just let me get some things together, would you like to drive?" "Well, Frances," I said, "I can't drive a stick, I mean I'm sure your car has a clutch, where I come from cars don't have clutches anymore, except sports cars, you just put them in drive and go." Again Frances and Iris looked at each other, but Frances agreed to drive. "Let me track down Tony first. I've got a week's vacation coming to me and I want it starting right now."

Chapter 18
Chad's Escort Service

Frances' car was a lovely light blue Cadillac. "Come sit up front with me, Chad," as Iris looked on, still scowling. It seemed like the hardest one to win over was going to be Iris.

"I've got a USO Victory benefit and a Bob Hope show to do this week," said Frances. "Why don't you accompany us to both of them? You could be our 'escort.' Jon is out of the country on location for a new picture. The studios often provide escorts for ladies who are single or whose husbands are unavailable. You'd get two for the price of one!" laughed Frances. "I've had some real stinkers," said Iris.

"Oh, don't mind her, Chad," said Frances. "How about it?"

"I'd very much like that, Frances, that's very kind of you," I said beaming. Wow, I thought, escorting Frances Langford to a big shindig like this! I must be dreaming. But then I realized Iris would be with us too. Oh well, I wasn't going to complain.

Frances looked me up and down. "First we'd better get you some 1945 clothes. You're going to cause quite a stir in Palm Springs dressed like that." I looked at my clothes. I had on a colored T-shirt and jeans, the uniform of the 21st century, but here I probably looked like an unemployed plumber.

"I'd let you borrow some of Jon's things," said Frances. "He's got more clothes than I do, but I think they would be way too big for you, especially the shirts. Better off with new."

"I appreciate this very much, Frances, I'll pay you back in 2007 money!"

"What did Tony say when you asked for a week off?" asked Iris. "Oh, you know Tony, he was fine, he knew about the benefit and he knew I had to do Bob's show anyway. He's such a dear! They're going to shoot around me, it won't hold up production." "I really appreciate all this, Frances, you're very kind, this is all like a dream to me," I said.

"Well, what do you think it is for me?" laughed Frances. "I don't get many visitors from the 21st century!" "That's for sure!" chimed in Iris. "All I ever get is 20th-century pests!" Frances and I both laughed at the quip but Iris remained stoic.

I asked Frances why she and her husband Jon Hall chose Palm Springs to live. I wondered if it had anything to do with that movie or "Will I Ever Know" She laughed and said, "No, we both like it and many of our friends live there."

At the mention of "Will I Ever Know," I noticed that her hands gripped the wheel tightly and there was that faraway look in her eyes again for a brief moment. It was apparent that the song meant as much if not more to her than it did me. A spell of silence followed; all of us seemed lost in thought. I was afraid of what Iris's thoughts were. I didn't feel any empathy at all from her. She seemed devoted to Frances and very protective, which was okay with me, but I just wanted an ally and I felt like I was making an enemy.

Chapter 19
Dressing The Part

"There's a Sanderson's department store," said Frances. "I have a charge a plate with them."

Charge a plate, I thought. I hadn't heard that term in years. My mother and aunt used to call them that even after charge cards came into vogue.

We parked and went inside—Iris too. She was sticking like glue. I knew why Iris was with us, but I so achingly wanted to spend some time alone with Frances. We went to the men's dept. and with Frances' approval I picked out a sport coat, slacks, and two shirts. Also, a pair of wingtip shoes. Frances told me I could borrow a couple of Jon's ties. Iris remained silent. I told the salesman I was wearing the outfit and to just pack up my old clothes with the extra shirt. He handled my old clothes as if they were from outer space; well, I guess in a way they were.

We also stopped in the cosmetic area. Frances wanted me to get a small can of pomade for that "slicked back" 1940s guy look. I couldn't wait! I went to the men's room and applied the pomade. Not sure how much to use, I put a huge wad on my hair and rubbed it in. It was then that I realized you didn't need much. My hair shone! Upon seeing me Frances exclaimed, "Quick, I need some sunglasses for the glare." Even Iris had to chuckle at all the grease. "Don't worry," said Frances, "we'll fix it when we get home, in the meantime let's get you a fedora to complete the package."

Will I Ever Know

I picked out a black fedora and tried to shape it like Humphrey Bogart's; I've always loved the 1940's fedora. "Say, you're not packing heat, are you stranger?" laughed Frances, as Iris just shook her head.

Once back in the car and heading towards Palm Springs, Frances started to quiz me on *The Bamboo Blond,* such as her co-star's name in the film, what was the name of the café they were dancing in, who else was in it. I answered each question correctly. I even threw in that the end would have Russell Wade pulling her into the kitchen while the group was singing around the piano. Frances and Iris looked astonished. "That's only one of several proposed endings," said Iris. "They can't decide on which one to use." "Well," I said, "that is the one they will use and it's damn cute too!" I continued, "I taped it off of the Turner Classic movie channel and…….oop." I then had to try and explain television and the machines known as VCRs. Both girls looked rather puzzled.

Chapter 20
Palm Springs

We arrived at Frances' home, a beautiful Spanish-style hacienda with a long driveway. We were met at the door by Edward, the butler. He was in full uniform and had the most wonderful British accent. I wondered if it was all real or if I was dreaming the whole thing. He looked like he came from central casting. Dora, the maid, was busy straightening up. Both appeared to be very efficient and knew their place.

"Edward," said Frances, "this is Mr. Chad Henson, an old friend who just, uh, dropped in unexpectedly, show him to the large guest room. Iris, you know where your room is." Dora, a small, unassuming woman, announced that dinner would be served within the hour. Iris and I went to our respective rooms to freshen up. I was pondering how I could get some of that pomade out of my hair without making a bigger mess.

I was shown to a room that was larger than my apartment, with large windows and big, billowy curtains. Edward opened the windows and in came a delightful scented breeze, far different than the gas fumes and pollution I was used to in my northeast Philadelphia apartment. The bed was a huge queen-size affair with large posts at the four corners. A huge closet occupied the other side of the room. It was so big I thought that a person could get lost in there. And this is the guest room, I thought. The master bedroom must be gigantic! There was a small balcony outside each window with a marvelous view of the property. I didn't tarry long, however; I wanted to get back to Frances before Iris came down.

Will I Ever Know

I descended the circular staircase, admiring the gorgeous pictures on the wall, all done in a South Sea motif. I knew Jon Hall had island roots and that he had made many of his adventure films on some exotic isles. It looked like he had tried to bring some of it to his home.

I found Frances sitting in the garden on a very plush sofa. The way the sun caught her hair, she looked just like an angel. "Frances," I gushed, "you are so incredibly beautiful!" Embarrassed, she put her head down and whispered, "Why thank you, Chad." Feeling awkward myself, I stammered, "I'm sorry, Frances, I didn't mean to get out of line, but it's so true, I…………." That's alright, Chad," she said. "You don't have to explain, dinner will be ready soon."

"There is so much I want to tell you," I said, "so many things you ought to know, I know I'm disrupting your life………." "It's okay, Chad, we'll have plenty of time to talk and sort all of this out." "But," I said, "and I mean no disrespect, it's going to be difficult with Ir………………."

"When do we eat, I'm starvin'" came a voice from just inside. It was Iris. Frances looked at me and smiled. "We're out here, Iris," said Frances.

Iris came out in a lovely pale blue gown; she obviously had clothes here because she hadn't brought anything from the studio.

I have to mention here that Iris Adrian and Frances were very good friends. Iris had taken Frances under her wing, so to speak, when Frances had first come to Hollywood a decade earlier. They'd made a couple of movies together and really hit it off. Although almost the same age, Iris was about a year older, and she looked on Frances as a little sister who needed her protection from the Hollywood wolves. She was instrumental in getting Frances together with Jon Hall. Frances had helped Iris recover from her divorce in 1936. Iris had remarried a couple of years later, but there was no sign of the second husband at this time. Iris had a rather cynical view of men and that was not helping me any.

"About 10 minutes Iris, hold your horses," said Frances. "It's not horses I want to hold," said Iris. "It's a knife and fork with some steak attached to them." "We're having roast beef," said Frances. "Chad, you're going to love Dora's roast beef. It's famous all over Palm Springs."

Chapter 21
Dinner Is Served

"Dinner is served," announced Dora in her small voice. We made our way into the large dining room. Candles were placed on the table, giving a surreal light to the room. Frances looked even more magical in the candlelight. Even though I was very hungry, I wasn't sure I could concentrate on food with that vision of loveliness sitting across from me.

The dinner, as promised, was magnificent. We each had a glass of Cabernet Sauvignon to start. The roast beef was so tender that you didn't need the knife. I'm no expert, but the silverware looked very old and very expensive. A tossed salad, mashed potatoes, and some sort of fancy string beans completed the setting. "We're plain eaters here, Chad," said Frances, "although both Jon and I are very fond of South Sea dishes." I knew that years later Frances would open up a Polynesian restaurant in Jensen Beach, Florida, but I chose not to bring that up. I amused and amazed the girls by telling them that I mostly ate frozen food from a box that was heated in a few minutes in a machine called a "microwave oven." Dora's roast beef, however, was much much much better. "I don't care where it comes from as long as it's food," chirped in Iris. Iris indeed did have a healthy appetite, although you'd never know it from her slim figure.

"How about that Russell Wade?" chimed Iris. "What a hunk! Doesn't he look great in that flyboy uniform? I predict he's going to be a BIG, BIG star! And that smile! OHHHHHHHH! I think he really likes you, Fran!"

Will I Ever Know

Russell Wade was Frances' co-star in *The Bamboo Blond*. Again I didn't say anything because I knew that Wade would continue to toil in obscurity in "B" movies, finally retiring from films in 1948 and making a fortune in real estate. He would develop the El Dorado country club in the mid-'50s and was the chairman of the Palm Springs golf tournament (now the Bob Hope Classic) there for many years. "Oh, Iris," said Frances, "Russell is a professional actor. You know he's devoted to Janie."

"Just the same," replied Iris, "I'd like to set MY cap for him!"

"Iris," cautioned Frances, "don't talk silly, your food is getting cold."

"OOP," said Iris, "can't let that happen."

The meal continued with more small talk; I was getting itchy to get Frances alone. After dessert of homemade apple pie and homemade ice cream, we were all full, even Iris.

"Let's have some coffee in the library," said Frances. "Dora, please bring the coffee into the other room." The room was magnificent, all dark-paneled, very expensive-looking wood. There was a mahogany desk, a very comfortable chair. Two sofas, four wingtip chairs, and a grand piano. "Chad, would you like a cigarette or cigar?" asked Frances.

"Well actually, I prefer a pipe," I said. "You know, it gives me that professorial, educated look, don'tcha know?"

"Jon likes a pipe once in a while, there's a jar of tobacco over on the desk and a rack full of pipes," said Frances.

"I brought my own," I said, showing them a Dr. Watson billiard pipe and a half-empty pouch of Captain Kidd tobacco, "but I'd like to try some of Jon's if I may." "Go right ahead," said Frances. "I love the smell of a pipe."

"Me too," chimed in Iris, "but I think I'll just light up a Cool Breeze." She grabbed a pack that was on the end table and lit up.

"I don't smoke," said Frances. "I'm afraid it might be bad for the voice."

"Honey, you got lungs like a horse," quipped Iris. "A little smoke ain't gonna bother you." We all laughed. Iris had a natural wit about her and despite the rather gruff exterior, she was really a sweet person. I just wished she liked me better. There was no name on Jon's tobacco, but it was a very rich aromatic blend that was absolutely delicious and very satisfying.

"Frances," I said after a while, "there's that huge, beautiful, white grand piano over there looking mighty lonely. Could you please sing us something? I know you never get asked," I chuckled.

"How about 'Night and Day'," suggested Frances. "Come on, we'll all sing."

Frances went to the piano, and Iris and I stood around her as she began. About 30 seconds into the song, Iris and I dropped our voices and just let Frances do her wonderful thing. She owned the song just as she owned everything she ever sang. That full rich voice, with that smooth, creamy lower register. The intricacies of Cole Porter held no terror for Frances.

After finishing "Night and Day," Frances started in on "Will I Ever Know." As she got to the line, "The moment that I see him I will know him, no matter how impossible it seems," she looked right at me and I began to melt.

We sang a couple more songs and continued our conversation. Iris asked some questions about the future. Remembering the professor's warning, I said that I really couldn't get specific about world and national events. I limited my answers to technology, which I considered safe. However, the skeptical look never left Iris's face. Before we knew it, it was almost 1 a.m.

"Well, gang," said Frances, "I'm going to bed. It's been a long day."

Iris and I echoed her sentiment. I wasn't all that tired but I was drunk on Frances. "How about a picnic tomorrow?" said Frances. "We can go up to the San Jacinto mountain area. It's lovely up there." "Fine with me," I beamed.

"Uh, you two go ahead, I have some, uh, shoppin to do. Might take all day. You know how it is, Fran, when I attack the stores."

"Are you sure?" said Frances. "It's a great spot for a picnic."

"Well, for once, honey, I'm not letting my stomach rule," said Iris.

Will I Ever Know

We all headed up the stairs to our respective rooms. Try as I might, I couldn't sleep. All I could think about was Frances. I thumbed through the memorabilia book with all the pictures I had collected of her. They didn't do her justice.

 She was much more beautiful in person.

Chapter 22
The Picnic And Iris Goes "Shopping"

I must have finally dozed off because the next thing I knew the sun was shining and I could smell bacon cooking. It was 8 a.m. so I quickly dressed and went down to the kitchen. Dora was cooking breakfast and Frances was working on the picnic basket. No sign of Iris yet.

"Good morning all," I chirped. "Good morning, Chad," said Frances, "I hope you slept well."

"Like the proverbial log" was my reply. "Where's Iris?" I asked. "Oh, she'll be down, she likes to sleep until at least 9," said Frances.

"I've got the picnic basket almost ready, I made sandwiches, packed some chocolate cake and a couple of apples."

"Thank you for the apples, Eve," I quipped.

"I hope you like cheese omelets and bacon," said Dora. "Oh yes I do" was my enthusiastic reply, "the perfect breakfast."

Halfway through the meal, Iris came bouncing in looking all dressed up for shopping, complete with hat and gloves in her hand. The typical way a woman would go out to shop in the '40s.

Will I Ever Know

"I'm starved," said Iris. "I haven't had a thing to eat all night!" Frances and I both laughed. Iris had this winning personality, always ready to put herself down. I just wished that she would accept who I was. But on the bright side, it looked like Frances had accepted me and I could feel us getting closer. At one point I touched her hand, which was so warm and soft. I felt myself feeling like the professor was sending me somewhere again, but fortunately it was only the power of love.

Frances was dressed very smartly in pants and a short-sleeve top, perfect for a picnic yet a little radical because women weren't wearing pants all that much yet.

Iris downed her omelet, bacon, orange juice, and coffee in the time it took me to butter my toast.

"Well, gang," said Iris, "I'm off. Frances, can I borrow the Caddy?"

"Sure, dear" was Frances reply. "The keys are in the top drawer of the table in the foyer."

"Okay, thanks, kiddo" was her snappy retort. "I gotta lot to do today!" And she was off.

Frances and I finished up our food and Frances said, "We can leave soon. I just want to freshen up, we'll take the roadster, we can have the top down." "Sounds good to me" was my more than enthusiastic reply.

In a few minutes, picnic basket in hand, we were out to the garage. The Halls had four cars: Frances' Cadillac, the roadster, a Packard touring car, and what looked like a '38 Plymouth that Edward used to run errands and Frances and Jon used when going incognito.

"What a beautiful day!" exclaimed Frances. "You're going to love the San Jacinto area. Many wonderful spots for a picnic."

I was dressed in my "1940s duds." I had washed my hair but there was still enough pomade left in it to give me that "shiny, smacked-down" look.

Frances grabbed the picnic basket and we were off to the garage.

"We'll take the Alfa-Romeo," said Frances. "Let's put the top down." I had never been in anything even remotely like an Alfa, so I was really excited.

Frances had her hair up in what I could only describe as a "beehive." I didn't know what they called it in 1945. The drive to the San Jacinto mountain area was wonderful.

Frances had a "moderately" heavy foot, taking the Alfa easily to 100 miles an hour in spots. The countryside was beautiful, the views spectacular, but I was concentrating on the beautiful scenery next to me. The golden hair shining in the sun, the beautiful profile, such perfect delicate skin. I'd never felt more alive, but was I? I was in 1945 and technically I wouldn't be born yet for almost 30 years. What would happen on July 20, 1973 if I were still here? I tried to put those thoughts out of mind as I lived my dream, speeding off to a picnic with the most beautiful girl in the world, any world.

We didn't talk much, since with the wind and sun in our faces it was hard to hear. I didn't care; this was paradise. Frances slowed up and declared, "Here's a good spot, we can take a long walk before lunch."

We had been driving about an hour. It was about 10:30. I secretly hoped it wouldn't be a LONG, LONG walk. I'm not the most athletic guy, and I wasn't sure if my 1945 shoes needed some breaking in. I should have worn the sneakers I'd come in.

As we started off, Frances said, "Let's take the basket with us, I know a really pretty spot a couple of miles from here." Being the gentleman, I carried the basket, wondering how much that would slow me down. I was also wondering if Frances had packed rocks in the basket because it was very heavy. I hoped this "dream" spot was closer than she had said.

After about 45 minutes and many shifts of the basket from one arm to the other, Frances exclaimed, "Here it is!" I looked up and saw what W. C. Fields would have called "an arboreal dell." An incredibly naturally cutout piece of land filled with trees and all sorts of flowers, a small body of water with a waterfall and several picnic tables. Arboreal dell indeed—this was Eden!

"Oh, Frances," I cried. "This is incredible!" "Isn't it, though," she said. "Jon and I have been here several times."

At the mention of Jon Hall, I came back to earth, sort of. Here I was in this beautiful romantic spot with another man's wife. The fact that they would divorce in 1955 assuaged my conscience a bit, but I couldn't help but wonder if I contributed in any way to the breakup down the road.

"Let's go on a little farther up the mountain, we can leave the basket here," said Frances.

That was welcome news for me, but I wondered how much further she intended to hike. If my 1945 shoes had been hush puppies, then the dogs were starting to bark. "Is it safe to just leave the basket here? Shouldn't we cover it up or something?" I asked. "No, it'll be fine, no one will bother it. Everything is wrapped well and there are no large animals to be curious about it," she said.

That's right; this is 1945, I remembered. Frances probably left her front door unlocked too. She took my hand and suddenly the barking dogs ceased and I was once more held captive by this enchanting creature. She was so beautiful I wondered if she was really human. In this setting, it reminded me of her 1941 film *The All American Co-Ed*, in which she sang the haunting song "Out of the Silence" in a beautiful outdoor grove. The song was nominated for an Academy Award. It lost out to *The Last Time I Saw Paris*. We walked for another 40 minutes or so up the mountain. We stopped to take in the beautiful view of the valley. I put my arm around her as we beheld the scene.

Chapter 23
Eden

I couldn't take it any longer. I pulled her closer to me and whispered, "Frances." I leaned over to kiss her but she pulled away.

"Not now, Chad, please, this is all happening so fast. Let's go eat our lunch." Dejected but not discouraged, I pulled away but took her hand. She didn't resist. We started back for the spot where we had left our picnic lunch. The walk back was quiet, subdued. I wondered if I had blown it. I kept thinking of "our" song, "Will I Ever Know." The line "Lips that are pressed to mine" kept going through my head in the marvelous way that Frances interpreted it on film and on records. Will my lips ever be pressed to hers? Usually being very awkward in romantic situations, I began wondering if I shouldn't have met up with Clark Gable first to get some pointers on how to be the "suave 1945 romantic." Too late for that you're on your own, Chad. Just relax and be yourself, I said to myself. That thought didn't encourage me either.

We got back to our "Eden," and our moods brightened just being in that wonderful spot. The basket was intact, untouched, and Frances began to spread things out. There was a nice picnic table under a tree. The basket seemed to have no bottom, as she produced enough food to feed the troops on one of her tours with Bob Hope.
"Whoa!" I said. "Are we expecting several thousand more people? I've never seen so much food for a picnic of two." "Well, I wanted to make sure you had enough. You look like a sandwich guy," said Frances.

64

Will I Ever Know

Normally, I love sandwiches. I used to think I was descended from the Earl of Sandwich, but being alone with Frances with the tension that was there, I wasn't hungry at all. There was chicken salad, tuna, meatloaf, chips, pickles, caviar— yes, caviar, which didn't thrill me but impressed me. There was a bottle of wine and also soda and water, chocolate cake, and apple pie.

I opened the wine and poured us each a glass. I made a toast. "To the trees!" I said; that's all I could think of.

I managed to eat a chicken salad sandwich, which was delicious, but it was a struggle to finish it. Frances picked at a meatloaf sandwich. I could tell she wasn't hungry either. I got up and stretched and walked around to Frances' side of the bench. "Come on, Chad," she said, "there's plenty more sandwiches, don't you like the food? I thought you'd have two or three done by now."

"The food is superb, Frances, everything is just perfect, I know this sounds cliché, but that's me, Mr. Cliché. I'd rather feast on your beauty."

Frances looked down and I thought I detected a slight blush.

I moved closer to her. I squeezed her hand and without saying a word, I turned her head towards me and planted a soft kiss. I moved back and then went in again. This time she resisted only slightly, whispering, "Chad, don't," but without much conviction. I kissed her again with a little more pressure. She fought back weakly but finally succumbed, kissing me back furiously. As the kisses became more ardent, it seemed as if all the frustration of the ages was being lifted. We groped each other, rather awkwardly at first, then fell to the ground in a warm embrace. "Let's go over to that grove of trees," I said breathlessly.

Even though there was no one around for miles, we were still out in the open. Once out of sight, our passion exploded as we explored each other, tearing each other's clothes off. As I undid my pants, I realized that my 1945 pants had a button-fly. How did they ever do it back then? Frances giggled as she tried to help me, but our hands kept getting caught in each others. Finally, the last button was undone and I was free. I took her gently to the ground and we started again. Her kisses were warm and vibrant; it was as if she were kissing my failures away—the divorce, the loss of my job, the other relationship disasters I had had. Her moans were soft and enticing. As we melded into each other, I felt as if my explosion could be heard for miles. Frances let out a long scream, on perfect pitch, and then we relaxed. Satisfied, I was happier than I can ever remember.

Breathlessly, Frances said, "Isn't this the time when we need a cigarette?" We both laughed.

"But what about you?" Frances continued. "You smoke a pipe." "That wasn't a pipe in my pants," I said. "I didn't bring one with me."

"Oh. I thought it was," laughed Frances. She continued, "I was thinking, what a big bowl on that pipe!"

We both laughed uproariously. It seemed as if all of the hesitancy, all of the reserve was gone now from Frances. We were both seeing each other in a different, more intimate light.

"What are you thinking?" asked Frances.

"'Will I Ever Know' is playing in my head, over and over," I moaned.

"The same with me," said Frances. "I know the answer to the question now."

We then embraced and kissed each other fervently, arousing each other again. This time it was slower, recalling the path we had just traveled and taking it again, exploring some little byways along the route, pausing to savor the joys and wonders along the way.

We took each other right up to the edge and would then back away, only to go further and further till we were at the very tip until suddenly we leapt into orgasm valley, flying as if we had wings of eagles. Then came the second explosion, mightier than the first but somehow more special. Spent, we rolled over.

Frances said, "Wow, what did you put in that pipe?" We both laughed and I hugged her until I thought she'd break. How could one woman be so passionate and so fragile at the same time? This little pixie who looks like she'd never got off the front porch has traveled the most remote places in the world with Bob Hope and the USO tours, fighting rare and tropical diseases, enemy gun fire, horrible living conditions, just to entertain and raise the spirits of our fighting forces. No wonder 3 million GI's were in love with her!

"Come on, Chad," said Frances playfully, "we better get going, it's going to take you a while to button those pants!"

"Why don't you help me?" I teased.

"Then we'll never get home." Frances winked.

"I'm not sure I ever want to leave this wonderful place," I said.

I was beginning to feel playful again, but I could see that Frances was anxious to get going. She had a USO benefit to rehearse tomorrow, the show itself the day after, and Bob Hope's show to do the night after that. She also had mentioned some possible rehearsals at home; bandleader Skinnay Ennis was possibly going to come over and run through some songs with her.

The ride back to Palm Springs was rather quiet. We were both lost in our own thoughts. Having sex frees the mind to think about other things, namely the consequences of what you've just done.

We hadn't used protection, so I began to fear what would happen if Frances got pregnant. First of all, it wouldn't be Jon's. Second, I didn't know what the child of a man who technically wasn't even born yet would be like. I thought of the professor having a major blowout fit if he knew. However, one look at Frances behind the wheel allayed my fears and I was once again entranced.

It was late afternoon when we got back to Frances' house. Frances fixed her makeup and hair in the garage. We didn't look too disheveled as we walked back into the house.

The Caddy wasn't back yet so I assumed Iris was still on her shopping spree.

"What time would you like dinner, Miss?" asked Dora. "Seven would be fine," said Frances. "Anything will do."

After our romp we had devoured most of the picnic lunch, having only picked at it before. Neither of us was very hungry, but I knew Iris would be ready for a full-course meal and then some.

"I'm going to change for dinner," said Frances. "Chad, make yourself comfortable in the library or freshen up if you'd like." I was as fresh as could be so I said, "I'll just go into the library and have a smoke."

Filling a pipe, I thought of Jon. It seemed like I was helping myself to more than just his tobacco. As I puffed away, I kept thinking about the events of the last few days.

Going to 1995, meeting the 82-year-old Frances, savoring the warm wonderful friendship we had, then going to 1945 and meeting and falling in love with the 32-year-old Frances. What did it all mean? What did I think would be the outcome? I had never thought all of that through before. My goal had been to meet Frances and form a relationship, but then what?

Frances came down, looking so lovely in a long, pale yellow gown, her hair piled on top of her head. It made her graceful neck look so appealing.

"Shall we go into dinner, Chad?" cooed Frances. "Certainly," I said, beginning to feel a little hungry but wanting to feast on Frances rather than the meal prepared by Dora.

"I hope you like Duck à l'Orange," said Frances. "Dora makes a divine duck." I had heard of it but had never tasted duck. My eating had always been very basic. A Wendy's combo meal was a gourmet feast for me. I decided I would pretend it was chicken.

Frances said grace and Dora proceeded to serve. It was very good actually, and it turned out I was hungrier than I'd thought. Frances took small delicate bites. It looked like she wasn't eating at all, but magically the food on her plate disappeared.

Chapter 24
Iris Returns From Her "Shopping Spree"

Midway through the meal, the front door opened and a shout came forth: "I'M BACK!!!!!" It was Iris back from her shopping spree. She had a few small packages, much less than I had figured.

"Iris," asked Frances, "looks like you didn't come home with much after all those hours at the stores."

"Uh, oh, well I had some other things to do," said Iris. "Come sit down and join us," invited Frances.

"I'm not that hungry," said Iris. "I'll just have Dora fix me a sandwich. Frances, I have to talk to you." Both Frances and I looked surprised as Iris went to the kitchen to place her order.

"I'll be upstairs," said Iris. Frances and I looked at each other, and then she said, "That was strange, I've never known Iris to come back from a shopping spree with so few items and not be ravenously hungry, I hope she's alright. I'll go up to her after we eat."

The meal continued, and we talked about the future. I told her some things that would happen that wouldn't turn the "cosmos into chaos," to quote the professor.

After our dessert of homemade pie and ice cream, Frances said, "Well, Chad, it's been a long day, I'm going to see to Iris and then go to bed."

"All right, my dear," I said. "Sweet dreams." I took her hand and kissed it, then gave her a long lingering goodnight kiss. We looked into each other's eyes, dreamily, both reliving the passion and love of the afternoon. We didn't say a word. We didn't have to. "Good night, darling," she said. "Good night, my love," I blurted out.

I watched her ascend the beautiful staircase, a vision of pure loveliness. My heart was racing, my resolve strong.

I determined to confront Jon Hall and declare our love to him. I also determined to stay in 1945, be with Frances, and stay away from Philadelphia where I would be born 28 years later. The craziness of it brought me back to earth for a moment. But I quickly returned to my own personal Shangri-la, thinking of my afternoon with Frances.

I sat in the library for a while, smoking and thumbing through some magazines, trying not to look at the beautiful wedding portrait of Frances and Jon hanging there. If I looked at it at all, I focused only on Frances, still a little ashamed to look Jon Hall in the face, even in a photograph.

Around midnight, I decided to head on up to bed. Frances had mentioned the three of us going to a lake tomorrow. She and Jon had a sailboat there. Iris would be with us, but I tried not to think about that.

In the back of my mind lurked two things. First, the professor and the Time Machine. I was sure he was back in 2007 trying to figure out how to screw me royally by bringing me back to the present. Second, Jon Hall. When was he due back? Would I be as bold and courageous in person with him as I was in my head?

I kept thinking of the song's words, "No matter how impossible it seems." That gave me courage.

As I went down the hall to my room, I could see the light was still on in Frances' room. I could hear two female voices talking very intently. Deciding not to stop in for a visit, I proceeded to my room and got ready for bed. Little did I know what was being said in Frances' room, and I was totally unprepared for what was to come in the morning.

Chapter 25
The Revelation

I slept fitfully, dreaming on the one hand of holding Frances in my arms, and on the other hand dreaming about being in between two worlds with the beautiful Frances on one side of me, and some horrible creature on the other side.

I awoke often, sweat-drenched and very hyper. Finally, dawn came and I lay there; the resolve and confidence were gone, being replaced by an anxiety so powerful it was unlike anything I had ever experienced.

I rose at 7:00, drained and exhausted, and got ready for breakfast.

It was a beautiful, sunny, cloudless day, like all the others in Palm Springs, but I felt neither sunny nor cloudless. I came down to breakfast and Frances was already there.

"Good Morning, your Loveliness," I chirped. "I hope you slept well." I leaned over for a kiss, but Frances turned her head so I got a mouthful of cheek.

"No, I didn't sleep very well at all," said Frances icily.

"Oh, I'm sorry to hear that," I said, getting more nervous by the second. I sat down to a dead silence, as Frances avoided looking at me.

Charles Henry

I tried my hand at some small talk—the weather, the meal, which was a beautiful concoction of scrambled eggs, bacon, and some other exotic ingredient that I couldn't determine.

Frances hardly touched her food. I was losing my appetite, too. Finally, I said, "Where's Iris?"

"I don't know," was her terse reply.

Now I was really nervous, just about jumping out of my skin. The Time Machine worry and the Jon Hall anxiety had been replaced by a much greater fear. Where was all the passion, excitement, and love of yesterday?

Finally, Frances broke the silence. "Chad," she said, "I want you to leave……….. NOW, no arguments, no persuading, I need you to leave." Immediately I was drenched in sweat—you know, the nervous stinky kind. I couldn't believe what I was hearing.

"No," I cried, "Frances, sweetheart, please don't do this!"

"Please, Chad," Frances said softly, "get your things, Edward will drive you back to L.A."

"What about yesterday?" I stammered. "What about the song, what about us finally meeting despite the disparity of time?"

"Edward will pull the car around, he'll be waiting out front. Goodbye, Chad!" And with that she got up and ran from the table, leaving me in a state of shock with my mouth wide open.

What is this? I thought. In trying to sort things out, I couldn't help but feel that Iris's absence from the table and that midnight bull session in Frances' room last night were tied together. But what had Iris said to her? What could she say to her? My world(s) were crumbling.

As I stood there, sorting out the tattered remnants of my broken life, in walked Edward.

"Sir?" he said. That was "Butlerese" for "Get your ass in gear, the car is waiting."

"Edward, give me a minute," I croaked. "I'm going to change my clothes, I'll be right

Will I Ever Know

down, I'll see you out front."

"Very good, sir" was his wooden reply.

I ran upstairs to my room, quickly changing out of my 1945 clothes and back into my 2007 duds. I didn't want anything from Frances. I didn't want to keep the clothes under false pretenses.

Now I was getting angry. Who does she think she is pulling this roller-coaster emotions act? Let me go back to the present and find a girl in my own time. After all, Frances is in reality 94 years old and dead to boot!

My senses were reeling. I was both angry and so in love with Frances at the same time. I was literally beside myself. I hung the clothes up neatly in the closet. I contemplated writing Frances a note.

Finding a pencil and a piece of paper, I wrote, "Dear Frances, my only love. I don't know what this is all about. I don't know what you found out or think you know about me, if anything. If I've done something to hurt you, I'm eternally sorry. I wouldn't hurt you for the world, any world. I hope you'll keep me in your thoughts and that in time they will be pleasant ones. The pain is unbearable. 'No Matter How Impossible It Seems.' Yours forever, Chad."

I left the note on the dresser, knowing Edward was waiting for me outside. Best to get out of here as quickly as possible. Stop the pain. Stop the pain was all I could think of.
I met up with Edward in the driveway, clutching my scrapbook. I couldn't bear to part with that, and left the house without looking back. From the second floor, if anyone had been looking up, a slight movement of the curtain in the front room could be detected. And there was the tear-stained face of the lovely Frances Langford watching the car pull away.

What was it that had turned Frances against me?

Chapter 26
Iris The Detective

Iris had not gone on a shopping spree the day of the picnic. She had gone on an investigative mission to find out who I really was and to expose me. Because of her devotion to Frances and the absurdity of my story, she was sure something foul was up.

She checked the L.A. phone book for my name and came up with a CHAD HANSON living in east L.A. Now, my name is Chad HENSON. Iris, poor girl, was never known for her spelling ability. Anyway, she drove into L.A. to the address in the phone book.

There was no answer at the apartment of this Chad Hanson, so she knocked for the superintendent of the building, Niko Popodopolous.

She knocked on the door and waited. The door slowly opened and she was met by overweight middle-aged, slightly balding, sweat-stained, T-shirt wearing man. The stench that emanated from the apartment made Iris slightly gag.

She asked the whereabouts of Chad Hanson. The super took his time replying, eyeing Iris up and down hungrily.

"Haven't seen him for three days, it's as if he just disappeared. He works at the grocery store, only two blocks down the street, maybe someone there can tell you where he is." Continuing to eye Iris up and down and smiling wickedly, he said, "You're welcome to come in and wait for him, no matter how long it takes. I'll keep you amused," he leered.

Will I Ever Know

"No thanks," said Iris, "I'm allergic to garbage." "Your loss, cookie," said the super.

Iris walked down to the grocery store and found the manager, T. J. Farnsworth.

He told her he hadn't seen him since last week and that his parole officer was looking for him too.
"Parole officer!" screamed Iris. "What did he do?"

"He served two years for fraud and passing bad checks," said the store manager. "He's on probation for three years. He is in deep doo doo. He was supposed to check in yesterday with his parole officer. Also, the police want to question him about the robbery at the jewelry store up the street last week. He matches the description given by two eyewitnesses. The owner was shot and is in serious condition. That's probably why he disappeared."

"Thank you VERY much," said Iris. "You've been a big help."

Armed now with ammunition against me, Iris couldn't wait to confront Frances with the news. But Iris was also concerned about Frances' safety, being out on a picnic with me, a paroled felon, a robbery and shooting suspect, or so she thought. It was during their late night session that Iris told Frances the news about Chad Hanson.

Frances went up to bed after dinner. She went right to her room only to find Iris waiting for her there.

"Boy, am I glad to see you," said Iris. "I was worried leaving you down there."

"Why, whatever do you mean?" said Frances.

"I'm going to cut right to the chase, dearie, this won't be pleasant. I did some digging today and your Chad is out on parole. He was jailed for fraud and passing bad checks, and he's wanted for questioning in a shooting at a jewelry store robbery. He has an apartment in East L.A. and works in a grocery store AND he's been missing since Sept 17th! The day he 'conveniently' dropped in on *The Bamboo Blond* set."

Frances turned white as a sheet, tears welling up in her beautiful eyes.

"Oh, honey," said Iris. "I'm sorry, I should have broke it to you more gently, but you know me. I'm so sorry."

"I don't know what to say," said Frances in a small voice. Then she burst into sobs. Iris went over and put her arm around her, trying to console her.

"It's better we find out now than later when your bank account is drained or, well, even worse."

"But Iris," sobbed Frances, "are you sure, are you really sure you got the right man? Did you describe him to them?"

"Yep, just under six feet tall, about a hundred and eighty pounds, medium build, dark brown hair. Both the grocery guy and the guy at the rooming house said that's him to a T." Frances was wringing her hands in agitation.

"I. . . I let that man do. . . oh, I can't think about it."

"Shall we call the police?" asked Iris. "No," said Frances, "I'm just going to tell him to leave in the morning, I'll have Edward drive him to L.A. and drop him off somewhere. If we call the police, there'll be a scene. Just think of the publicity, the investigation, I can't handle that right now."

"I see what you mean, Fran, best to just get him out of the house and away from you, they'll catch up with him eventually."

"Oh, Iris, what am I going to do? Everything's ruined, my dreams, the song, say. . . what about 'Will I Ever Know,' how did he know about that, how did he know about the effect it had had on me?"

"Well," said Iris, "he probably spent a lot of time getting to know all about your career. Got familiar with all your songs, specially the obscure ones, I gotta admit those words is deep for 'Will I Ever Know,' but listen, dearie, be glad you found out now. Remember that. Just concentrate on the show. The boys are countin' on you."

"Oh, Iris," sobbed Frances, "how can I concentrate on the USO show with all of this going on?"

Will I Ever Know

"Look," said Iris, "I'm sorry to have dumped all this on you, you know me and how 'delicately' I put things, I should have tried to soften the blow."

"That's okay, Iris," said Frances. "I know you were only thinking of my welfare, I'm a big girl, now please, I'd like to be alone."

"Sure, honey, I'll be in my room if you need me." Iris left the room and Frances began a new round of sobbing.

Chapter 27
Dora And Edward

"Edward," whispered Dora. "What's going on? Miss Frances seems awfully upset, she's dismissed Mr. Henson and after they went on that picnic yesterday."

"I have no idea, Miss Frances came to me early this morning and told me to drive Mr. Henson into the city right after breakfast and drop him, in her words, at a hotel or someplace. She didn't specify."

"Strange goings-on indeed," said Dora, "and I wonder why Miss Iris didn't go with them on that picnic?" And Miss Frances a married woman and all. I tell you, Edward, in my day we wouldn't tolerate such shenanigans."

"Now, Dora, remember this is 1945, times are different, the war has changed a lot of things."

"Common decency don't change," said Dora haughtily. "I think of poor Mr. Jon so far away from home, with no idea what's going on here."

"Nothing's going on, Dora, for heaven's sake, Mr. Henson's an old friend of theirs."

"HMPH," said Dora, "the next time Mr. Jon meets Mr. Henson will be the first time, says I."

Will I Ever Know

Edward said, "Mr. Henson seems a little down on his luck, I think I'll give him some money to make sure he can get a hotel room."

"Do what you like, Edward, you know what they say about a fool and his money."

"Just clear the table and get those dishes done" was his reply.

Chapter 28
Exiled In Los Angeles, Edward Finances Me

Edward had dropped me at a hotel in downtown L.A. "What are you going to do, sir?" he asked.

"I don't know, Edward," I replied. "I have no money, no job. Maybe I'll try to break into the movies. I've always been a frustrated actor. Or maybe I'll get a job as a dishwasher. That's probably more my speed and steadier work."

"Take this, sir, please." And he handed me some folded up money.

"Oh, no, Edward, I couldn't" was my reply. "You don't have to do that."

"I insist, sir," he said. "I don't know what happened between you and Miss Frances, but I can't help but feel it was all a misunderstanding. I know she wouldn't want you left destitute."

"Thank you, Edward," I said. "I really appreciate it." We shook hands and he left. He was right—I was destitute. Even though I had a pocketful of money, it was 2007 money. If I tried to use it, I'd probably be arrested for counterfeiting.

I opened the bills Edward had given me. There were five twenty-dollar bills. A hundred dollars; God bless Edward for his thoughtfulness.

Will I Ever Know

The hotel was a little shabby but not run down. It wasn't the Ritz, but it wasn't skid row either. It was the Royal Arms.

I asked the desk clerk about a room and was informed it was $10 a week paid in advance. Ah, 1945 prices! I could probably get a steak dinner for 75¢, but I wasn't sure if steak was still being rationed. Oh well, I wasn't hungry anyway.

I went up to room 945. How ironic. I was in 1945, and the room number was 945. The room was small but clean, with a bed, of course, a small chest of drawers, a chair, and a small sink. The bathroom was down the hall. Not too enchanted about that.
A small window gave me an excellent view of the brick building next door. Where was the flashing neon sign?

I had nothing really to put away as I had left the 1945 clothes back at Frances' house. Maybe she could return them to the store. Maybe she'd give them away. Maybe she'd burn them. Maybe I didn't really care. I didn't want anything from her.

My sadness was now turning to anger once again. Whatever had turned her against me? What really hurt was that she didn't give me a chance to explain or defend myself. Women! 1945 or 2007, they were all the same. My ex-wife was the same way. I guess that's one of the reasons she was my ex-wife.

Well, enough philosophizing and pity-partying. I was here in 1945, and I needed to get a job. $100 was not going to last long even in this era. I reached for my wallet to put the now $90 into it, but it wasn't there! Oh, great, I must have left it in my 1945 clothes back at Frances' house. Well, it wasn't going to do me any good anyway; credit cards were no good here, and I couldn't use the driver's license for anything. It all linked me to 2007. Better off without it. Frances could keep it as a souvenir—HAH!

I set out to find a newspaper and check out the want ads. I hoped I didn't look too conspicuous in my T-shirt and jeans. Jeans were dungarees back then and a T-shirt.......... well, a T-shirt is a T-shirt. I put the scrapbook away in one of the drawers. I still had it. I wanted to get rid of it but I just couldn't.

Frances Langford. . . I was very angry with the 1945 Frances Langford, but I still fondly remembered my time with the 1995 Frances Langford. How warm and wonderful she was. Oh well, the more I thought about it, the crazier I felt. Off to the newsstand and hopefully off to work!

Chapter 29
Job Hunting And Frances Copes

I got the paper and went to the luncheonette next store for some breakfast. I really needed some coffee! Going right to the want ads, I scanned them quickly. There were a lot of temporary jobs. That might be an option. I didn't know how long I'd be here.

I began to worry about being whisked out of 1945. I hated to leave under these conditions. Despite trying to be angry and "done" with Frances, I couldn't stop thinking about her. How could I make this right? How could I make this right when I didn't even know what was wrong?

After breakfast, my first stop was not at a perspective employer, but the local thrift store. I needed some authentic clothes if I was going for interviews. There was one just across the street.

They had tons of used clothing in various stages of wear. I picked out a dark brown suit, a couple of dress shirts that weren't frayed, and a couple of decent looking ties; also, a pair of black shoes in very good condition. Their stock of brown shoes was very low and not in good shape, and there were none in my size. Hopefully, I could upgrade once I got a job.

Decked out in my new togs, I was ready to pound the pavement. I started out with clerical white-collar positions. I seemed to make good impressions, but the snag came in when they asked for references and experience. Value Barn didn't exist. I didn't exist. I left those items blank on the application forms and was told they would "be in touch with me," which I felt was business language for "don't let the door hit you in the ass."

I hit a law firm, Dudley, Williams, Goldberg, and Stronsky, to apply for a law clerk job. I knew nothing about law, but I did know how to file.

I was seated in the office of a Mr. Galen Peabody, who was the Assistant Personnel Director.

As I waited for Mr. Peabody, I glanced at the pictures on his desk. There he was with Mrs. Peabody, and there were individual photos and a group picture of four children, two boys and two girls who I assumed were the "little" Peabody's.

But the picture next to his phone really caught my eye. It was an 8x10 picture of Frances, and inscribed "To Galen, Warmest regards, Frances Langford." I couldn't get away from her, not that I really wanted to.

Mr. Peabody came into the office. "Hello, I'm Galen Peabody, welcome to Dudley, Williams, Goldberg, and Stronsky." He had a firm handshake and appeared to be very polished.

"I'm Chad Henson, I'm here about the law clerk job," I said.

"Ah, yes, are you just back from the military?"

"No, I'm new to Los Angeles, just arrived a few days ago. I don't have any military service." Which was true, I had not been in the service; in fact, I had never even considered it.

"Hmm," he said, frowning a bit, "I see." I could tell that hadn't won me any points at all.

"Well, here is our standard application form, fill it out, leave it with Miss Duffy at the desk, and we'll be in touch with you." He gave me that look of "you don't stand a ghost of a chance." I figured I'd try a little "schmoozing."

"Mr. Peabody," I said, "I couldn't help noticing that gorgeous picture of Frances Langford on your desk. I'm a big fan. I think she is fabulous!"

He brightened. "Yes, she is wonderful. I got that picture when I was in the South Pacific, saw her in one of Bob Hope's USO tours. She was giving out these photos and signing all of them. I waited in line an hour and a half to get this one. She was tireless. She stayed until she ran out of pictures. Those who didn't get pictures were told to write her at Command Performance. Everybody who wrote eventually got one. She's even more beautiful in person." How well I knew THAT! "Thank you for your consideration, Mr. Peabody."

"You're welcome I'm sure," he said.

I left his office, hoping that I had scored a little in his favor. I went out into the reception room and filled out the application, leaving blank my work history and references, tempted to put Frances' name in the reference column but resisting that temptation. After I'd finished, I gave it to Miss Duffy, who promptly put it on top of a huge pile of other applications. I thanked Miss Duffy and left.

I had now exhausted the white-collar jobs and started on the other more mundane ones. Truck driver was out, as was cab driver, because I couldn't drive a stick shift.

I was getting tired and it was close to four o'clock. I figured it was time to quit, as most places were probably getting ready to close for the day. I'd get a fresh start in the morning. I sat down on a bench and started to thumb through the rest of the paper. Getting to the entertainment section, there it was: "USO VICTORY BENEFIT"

There was a picture of Frances, Bob Hope, and others who were appearing. Duke Ellington, Frank Sinatra, Billy Eckstine, Ella Fitzgerald, Mickey Rooney, Eddie Cantor, and on and on. I began to feel an overwhelming sadness. I was supposed to go to this show. And now, I was sitting on a transit company bench in thrift-store clothes, looking for a job. Any job.

My heart was aching for Frances, but my stomach was also crying, "feed me, feed me." So I found a modest restaurant and had a modest chicken dinner. I then made my way back to the Royal Arms. I figured I'd turn in early, get an early start in the morning. I took a long shower and, feeling very relaxed (well, "tired" would be a better word), plopped onto the rather rickety bed and examined the events of the day. In a few minutes, I was asleep.

Frances was up early and getting ready to do a rehearsal for the USO show. She spent some time in the library going over her songs on the piano. She was to get about a half an hour with the band that afternoon, if that. With so many acts on the program, rehearsal time was very limited.

"I'm ready, Iris, let's go."

"How ya doin', honey?" asked Iris.

"I've been better," said Frances icily. "I just hope I can concentrate on the show, I'm liable to forget the words or something to my songs."

"Don't be silly, sweetie, you been singin' them songs for years, you know 'em forward, backward, and sideways."

"How about the songs they're having me do?" she said with a sarcastic laugh. "They're having me do 'At Last' and 'You made Me Love You,' now there's two big laughs. I wonder who the joker was who picked them out? I'd like to get my hands on him and. . . and. . . Ohhh." Frances started to break down again, but regained her composure. "Let's just get going!"

"Right with you, Fran," said Iris nervously.

I awoke still feeling tired and listless. The thought of another day of job hunting didn't thrill me, but it had to be done.

After a quick breakfast and a fresh newspaper, I was off again. There seemed to be a need for dishwashers in 1945 Los Angeles, as there were many listings for them in the want ads.

By noon I had gone to seven restaurants, been turned down flatly by four of them, and had left applications at three of them. This was very discouraging. I decided to break for lunch. I hoped that maybe the little luncheonette I had picked out might need a dishwasher, cashier or something. The Koffee Korner was the one I picked. Here's hoping……………..

Chapter 30
I Find A Job And Frances Rehearses

The auditorium was crowded with celebrities lined up for the big USO VICTORY BENEFIT show. With the end of the war just a week ago, this was thrown together hastily but had the support of most of the major stars in the entertainment world. Most performers were doing things they had done for years because rehearsal time was short.

The rehearsals were spread out over three days, with some even being held the morning and afternoon of the show. Frances and Iris were scheduled for the second day. Iris was going to rehearse a sketch with Jack Carson and Phil Silvers in one of the small rooms off the main hall. Frances was going to rehearse with a small studio band in a smaller auditorium.

Howard Bartlett was an assistant bandleader who would direct the rehearsal for Frances. Because Frances knew and had performed her songs so often, she was not rehearsing with the show band and Skinnay Ennis, the bandleader. Frances had worked with Skinnay for years, so she really didn't need much rehearsal.

"That was fine, Fran," said Howard. "I don't think we need to do any more."

"I'm sorry, Howard," said Frances. "I'm a little out of sorts today, I'll be ready tomorrow."

Will I Ever Know

Frances had sort of limped her way through the renditions of "At Last" and "You Made Me Love You," but her timing and pitch were perfect. Howard Bartlett was satisfied, feeling that the adrenaline would flow the night of the show. Frances just hadn't been able to put any "oomph" into the songs.

Frances waited for Iris to be through with her sketch outside of the rehearsal room. She greeted some people, making a little small talk, but was anxious to get going. She really wanted to be alone. Iris came out of the room, and Frances gave her a "Let's go." And off they went for home.

"We had a good time in there," said Iris. "We're going to ad-lib some of it, those guys are great!"

Frances was driving and half listening; she felt like she was in some sort of bad dream and was desperately trying to wake up.

Dora had dinner ready when they got home. Frances and Iris ate in silence. You could have cut the gloom with a knife.

Iris, trying to start some kind of conversation, said, "Have you heard from Jon? He should be home soon, shouldn't he?"

"Iris, you know Jon almost never writes when he's on location. I sent him a couple of letters but I've gotten no answer. I have no idea when he'll be back."

"Oh" was all Iris could think of to say. Dinner over, Frances said, "I'm going to turn in early, we have a big day tomorrow. Sorry I haven't been better company, honey, tomorrow's another day."

"That's okay, Fran, get a good night's sleep." Sleep, thought Frances; I'll probably toss and turn the whole night. She made her way up the stairs.

The Koffee Korner was a very small eatery with a small counter, a few booths, and a couple of tables. Red-and-white-checked tablecloths decorated the booths and tables. Apparently, this was a "one man" operation because that's all I saw working.

The man was Justus Campbell, an energetic guy about my age. He, in turn, was taking orders, doing the cooking, and working the register. It wasn't very busy, so it didn't take too long to get my food. As he left the check, I had an idea.

"Looks like you could use some help," I said.

"You got that right, man," he said. "I had somebody but he walked out the other day, wanted more money. I just couldn't give it to him. I'm barely making it as it is. It's not easy for a black man in this city to make a go of a business. I sunk everything I had into this place, my savings, a small inheritance I got from my grandmother. All I dreamed about while I was in the service was having my own restaurant. Well, I got it but I don't know for how long. My wife Susie is going to have a baby so she can't work right now. Things is lookin' bad."

"Say, uh. . . " "Justus, Justus Campbell." "Uh, Mr. Campbell, I need a job, bad, I don't require much, if I don't get a job soon, they'll throw me out of my room. I can do almost anything but cook, but I could do the waiting on and the register, I'll even do the dishes at night."

I couldn't believe I was offering to do all that; remember my "delicate balance between inactivity and sloth."

"Mister, you musta been sent from heaven! I'm about wore out! You're. . . " "Henson, Chad Henson." "Pleased to meet you, Mr. Henson, you're hired!" Yippee! I thought. It had worked out just as I'd hoped it would. Desperate man, no application, no references, just work and a paycheck.

"We'll split the tips if it's okay with you, Chad, I'm really hurtin'."

"That's fine with me," I said, "and I thank you."

"Listen, Chad, I have to close early today, gotta go to the bank, some cat wants to see me about the loan, hope there's not a problem. Can you be here at 5:30 a.m.? We can set up and be ready for the 6:30 crowd." "Sounds good to me, see you then."

Well, I had a job. That was the main thing. I needed to really get to bed early if I was going to be there at the Koffee Korner at 5:30 in the morning. Salary hadn't been discussed but I didn't care. I had a job with tips; that was the main thing.

Chapter 31
Vindication

Back at Frances' house, it was early in the morning.

The big USO benefit was only hours away. Frances was cried out for the moment. She rose from her bed and began wandering aimlessly around her room, looking out the window at nothing, pacing.

She left her room and walked down the hall to the room I had stayed in. She paused at the closed door, then opened it and slowly looked around. Dora had made the bed and straightened up, so all traces of Chad Henson had been removed.

Seeing a piece of paper on the floor, Frances picked it up. It was the note I'd left her. She read it and a new wave of tears started. The tears gave way to anger. She crumpled the paper into a small ball, but instead of throwing it out, she put it in the pocket of her robe.

She began to cry again, falling on the bed in muffled sobs, hoping to get some of my essence, I suppose.

Her eyes drifted to the closet and she saw my 1945 clothes hanging there. Memories flooded her mind as she thought of the fun time we'd had in the store picking out my outfit, the pomade, the songfest we'd had after dinner, the glorious time spent in our "personal Garden of Eden" at the picnic. The warmth, the passion we shared at that spot. She began again to sob hysterically.

She ran to the closet and embraced the clothes, achingly wishing that I was there wearing them. As she embraced the jacket, she felt something in the inside pocket. In my hasty departure, I had left my wallet in the jacket. Slowly, she withdrew it and opened it up. She thumbed through the credit cards, not really knowing what they were. There was no money. I don't keep money in my wallet but prefer to jam it in my pants pocket, which can be chaotic and interesting at the same time.

She found my driver's license, which had fascinated her at my arrival. The picture on it made her cry even more. She read and reread all the data on the license, CHAD HENSON M 5' 11" 175. She looked back at the name; she said it over and over again, "CHAD HENSON, HENSON HENSON HENSON HENSON. . . " Suddenly the light bulb went on in her head.

"IRIS IRIS!" SHE SCREAMED. "IRIS, COME IN HERE QUICKLY!!"

"Where are you?" came Iris's muffled reply.

"I'm in Chad's room, come here quickly!" Iris burst into the room. "Frances, are you alright, what's wrong?"

Frances stood there with a wild look in her eye that startled even the jaded Iris Adrian.

"Frances, what is it?"

"Iris," said Frances very slowly and deliberately, "what is his last name? SAY IT!"

Befuddled, Iris said, "Hanson, Chad Hanson, what is this all about?" "SPELL IT............... NOW!!!!!"

"Uh, H-A-N-S-O-N, I guess," said Iris. "You know I ain't that good at spelling."

"Hanson," repeated Frances, "Henson, Hanson, Henson, Hanson." Frances began to laugh and cry at the same time.

"Honey, you better lie down, I'm gonna call the doctor," said Iris, very concerned.

Will I Ever Know

"NO NO NO, don't you see, his name is not HANSON, it's HENSON, look at his driver's license." "Well, uh, sweetie, I don't mean to burst your bubble but this could be a fraud too," said Iris meekly.

"I know," said Frances, "but we owe it to Chad to be sure. Do you remember where this Chad Hanson lived? We've got to show this picture to the building superintendent and the grocery store manager. They'll be able to tell if it's our Chad or not."

"But Frances, you have the USO show tonight."

"Just throw my gown in the backseat, we've got to get to L.A. Now!"

I was up bright and early for my new job. I liked Justus Campbell. He seemed like a decent, hard-working man. I truly hoped I could help him.

I got to the Koffee Korner at 5:15 and was met by a sign in the window. CLOSED UNTIL FURTHER NOTICE. My heart dropped. Mr. Campbell must have gotten bad news yesterday at the bank. I knocked on the door anyway, calling out his name, but there was no answer. Dejected, I was out of a job that I hadn't even started. Back to the want ads.

I bought a paper and sat on a park bench to wait for business hours, grabbing a quick cup of coffee and a doughnut from a vendor. I wondered if he needed any help.

The day ended up as it had begun—no job. Apparently, even for a dish washing job in Los Angeles, you needed references. I was very tired. Before going back to the hotel I stopped at a fairly expensive restaurant not on my list. They didn't need any help either

Frances and Iris pulled up at Chad Hanson's rooming house. Rushing into the building and knocking at the super's door, they were greeted by the same fat, balding, semi-shaved, middle-aged man. "Well, well," said Popodopolous as he looked at Iris, "you're back, I guess you liked what you seen, heh heh, and you've brought a friend." He was eyeing Frances up and down. Frances cut right to the chase, showing him the picture on my driver's license. "Is this Chad Hanson?" she asked.

"Why don't you both come in and we can talk about ol' Chad" was his leering response.

"Listen, Mr. Popodopolous, we ain't got time for chitchat, is this or isn't it Chad Hanson?" was Iris's terse question.

Looking at the picture but looking more at the girls, he said, "Naw, that ain't him. Chad's got kinda a horsey face, you know, like lean."

"Thank YOUUUU very much," cried Frances.

"Why don't yous come in and wait for him, I can make it very cozy for the three of us."

Staring intently at Frances, he said, "Say, you look like that dolly Frances, uh, what's her name?" Before he got the words out, Frances and Iris had run back to the car and were headed for the grocery store where this Chad supposedly worked. "LANKFORD, THAT'S IT, that's that dame's name, Fran Lankford, right here in my apartment, well well, ain't that something? Shoulda had my camera handy. Ain't nobody gonna believe this!"

"I hope it's still open," said Iris. "It's getting late." "One down, one to go," chirped Frances. They pulled up to the grocery store just as it was closing for the day.

"Hey, mister, remember me?" shouted Iris. "Wait a minute, just one question" as they barreled their way into the store.

"I'm sorry, ladies, we're closed for the day," said the manager, T. J. Farnsworth. "Please," said Frances, "just one question. Is this Chad Hanson? She showed him the photo. Farnsworth peered at the picture on the driver's license.

"Oh my, no," said Farnsworth emphatically. "Hanson doesn't look at all like this. He's got jet-black hair." (Mine was that sort of indescribable brownish color.) "Still haven't seen him, do you want to leave a name or phone number where he can get in touch with you?"

"That's okay," said Frances jubilantly, as the girls both turned and ran from the store. "You've been most helpful!"

"If you find him, tell him he's fired!" shouted an agitated Farnsworth.

Frances went to the phone booth on the corner and called the house.

Will I Ever Know

"Edward, what's the address of the hotel where you dropped Chad?"

"It's the Royal Arms on Santa Monica."

"Good," said Frances, "that's not too far from where we are, thanks, Edward."

Frances wrote down the address and she and Iris jumped into the car, headed for the Royal Arms.

Chapter 32
I Am Rescued

"Step on it, Iris," yelled Frances. "Okay, okay, keep your shirt on, girlie, I don't wanna get pulled over, I got two tickets pending already."

"Just GOOOO," said Frances excitedly. My hotel was a few blocks uptown, right in the heart of the city. It was rush hour to boot. Rush hour in L.A., 1945, was no better than it is today.

Finally, arriving at my hotel, they quickly parked the car and ran into the hotel.

"Chad Henson, please," said Frances, "what's his room number?" The clerk looked up from his movie magazine and said, "I'm sorry, Mr. Henson is out, I don't know when he'll be back. You can wait here in the lobby for him if you like."

"Thank you," said Frances, "we'll be over here."

"SAYYYYYYYYYYY," the clerk exclaimed, "aren't you Frances Langford?"

"No," said Frances, "I get that a lot. I don't know what the big fuss is about Frances Langford. I think I'm much better-looking than she is, and I can sing better too!"

Frances sat down with Iris and they both giggled. The clerk went back to his magazine but kept peering over the top of it, not quite sure if he was being put on.

Will I Ever Know

Finally, there was the hotel. My dilemma was, should I have something to eat first or go freshen up? The need to freshen up won over my hunger, so I went right to the hotel. As I went through the revolving door, I thought I was hallucinating. Maybe it was the hunger? But sitting in the lobby were Frances and Iris!

"OH CHAD!!!!!!!!!!!!" screamed Frances as she leapt from the chair and threw her arms around me, laughing and crying at the same time. "Oh darling, I'm so sorry." Iris came over and said, "Me too, buddy, me too, I know I haven't treated you fairly."

I thought I was dreaming. The room seemed to spin as I fervently kissed Frances and held her very tight.

"Uh, could somebody bring me up to date? I feel like I've missed something."

"Oh darling," said Frances, "it was all a terrible misunderstanding, you see……………"

"Hold on, Frances, let me explain, it's all my fault. You see, Chad, I've been very suspicious of you from the beginning, in case you haven't noticed"—little nervous giggle there—"I'm very protective, I guess too protective of Frances. She's the little sister I never had. Anyways, I just felt that you were out to take advantage of her or bilk her out of some money, whatever………………."

"Hey, gang," said Frances, "we have to get going, I'm due at the USO benefit. Chad, I have my gown in the car. Before you check out, and you are checking out and going to the show with us, may I use your room to change?"

"Of course," I said. "I'll take you up there." Iris had gone out to the car and was standing there with the gown.

Frances and I took the elevator up while Iris went over to the befuddled desk clerk. "Say, buddy, how much do you want for that snazzy sport coat? I'll give you twenty bucks for it."

"Why, why, I don't know," said the clerk, "what could you possibly want with my jacket?"

"Well, to tell you the truth"—Iris leaned over the desk very confidentially—"I run a clothing museum down on La Cieniga Boulevard. And this jacket would fit beautifully in my current exhibit. It's a great example of 20th-century 'Clerkus Hotelus.' How about it? Twenty smackers."

The coat had probably cost him no more than $10 or $15 in 1945 dollars, so here was a chance to make five bucks and have the coat on "exhibit."

"Alright, I suppose, make it $22 and it's a deal." "Deal," said Iris as she gave him the $22 and took possession of the jacket.

I waited outside the room while Frances changed, still reeling from my turn of fortune. The door opened and out stepped a heavenly vision in a light-blue, off-the-shoulder formal gown. Her hair flowed down to her shoulders and parted slightly in the middle to form that "V-for-victory" hairstyle so popular during the war years. She was indescribably beautiful.

I gulped, swallowing my adam's apple. "Oh, Frances," I gushed, "you are a vision of loveliness."

"Why thank you, dear, but we have got to go, now."

She raced down the hall to the elevator, me trailing after her. In the elevator, I put my arm around her and she looked up at me with that billion-dollar smile. We were going down, but I was ascending to the heavens.

Iris was waiting for us at the door, holding a jacket and a bag of sandwiches. There was no time to eat dinner.

As we rushed past the desk, the clerk yelled out, "HEY, you ARE Frances Langford!!!!!" Frances turned and smiled at him as we went out the revolving door. Iris said, "Here, Chad, put this on."

"Where did you get that?" I said.

"Oh, I gave the clerk $22 bucks for it. It'll make you look more like a dressed-up 1945." My thrift store suit looked rather pathetic next to these two glamour girls. Since we were going to this gala USO benefit, this tan blazer would make me look a little more dressed up.

Will I Ever Know

I, however, removed the name pin "Melvin" from the pocket. "Thank you, Iris, that was very thoughtful."

"I'm on your side now, kid," winked Iris.

Iris drove, while Frances and I were in the backseat. We devoured the sandwiches in no time. Frances had a chinchilla wrap around her shoulders that was so soft and beautiful. We held hands just like two teenagers. Iris drove rather fast but managed to almost stay within the speed limit.

Chapter 33
The USO Benefit Show

W e were at Hollywood and Vine in a few minutes. A valet took our car and we three marched in together amidst flashing light bulbs and reporters shouting questions. Things haven't changed much. Frances and Iris were beaming. I was trying to remember to smile, but I was in a dazed state what with the turn around of events, so I probably looked like a deer in the headlights.

Frances and Iris headed backstage. Frances called over an usher and told him to put me in a seat in the VIP section.

"We'll see you after the show," said Frances. "Come backstage, use this door over here, and give the usher this." She handed me a little ticket-like thing that said "Authorized backstage pass F. Langford." This would ensure that I had easy access to the backstage area. She kissed me lightly and she and Iris were off.

Iris was dressed in a very business-like suit. She was doing that office comedy sketch with Jack Carson and Phil Silvers.

The usher took me over to the VIP section. I was in the middle of the third row—a great seat. The show was starting. We had just made it. The seat next to me was empty. The house lights were going down. Applause as the emcee for the evening, Ken Niles, took the stage. This was so exciting; I wished I had a video recorder! All of a sudden I felt a plop next to me, and when I looked over, it was old ski nose himself, Bob Hope.

"Excuse me," he said, "my dog sled was late picking me up." We both laughed and settled in for the show. I'm sitting next to Bob Hope, I thought to myself. WOW. After several musical and comedy numbers. . .

It was time. . . time for Frances. Ken Niles had the orchestra do a drum roll. . . "And now here's a young lady you all love, a world traveler, she's logged more miles entertaining the troops than any five other people combined, the lovely, talented FRANCES LANGFORD!" The band played a flourish as the audience erupted into applause and whistles, Bob Hope next to me leading the charge. She gracefully swept onto the stage, all smiles, and started to sing. . . "At last, my love has come along, my lonely days are over, and life is like a song."

As she sang those opening lines she was looking right at me, as if those words were meant to describe her feelings about our love.

After the song was over, the audience showered her with shouts of "bravo." As she left the stage, she threw me a little kiss.

"Say," said Bob Hope, "do you know her?"

"Uh, yeah, we're uh, old friends, I, uh, you see I just dropped in for a visit."

"Oh," said Hope, "by the way, I'm Bob Hope, glad to meet you."

"I'm Chad Henson" was my reply. "The pleasure is all mine, Mr. Hope."

"Bob, Chad, Bob, Mr. Hope is my father." He chuckled.

It was intermission. Frances had another number to do in the second half, and Bob was going to make an unexpected guest appearance.

"Got to go. What's a USO show without Hope?" he said as he left for backstage.

I didn't know what to do. Should I go backstage? It would probably be a madhouse back there, and by the time I found Frances it would be time for the show to resume. Frank Sinatra had just arrived. He went right to the backstage area since he was going to do a number in the second half. The place was crawling with celebrities.

The lights were flashing: time for Act II. Bob Hope's seat was empty since he had gone backstage to do his "surprise" guest spot. An older, dignified lady was led to the vacant seat. She looked familiar; then it hit me, it was ETHEL BARRYMORE! I was somewhat embarrassed; I felt rather dorky in my tan hotel blazer, thrift-store shirt and tie, and brown pants.

After being seated, Ethel Barrymore looked at me and said, "How do you do?" I was flabbergasted! Ethel Barrymore greeting me!

"Oh, Ms. Barrymore," I gushed, "so nice to meet you, my name is Chad Henson."

She had one of those lorgnettes, you know, glasses on a stick that were so popular with "mature women" in those days. She eyed me up and down. "What did you call me, young man?"

Oops, I had called her MS. Barrymore and dear Ethel, still keen of ear, had picked it up. I was 30 years ahead of time. In 1945, no one knew what a "MS." was. Think, Chad, think! "Uh, MISS Barrymore, so sorry, I have a bit of a speech impediment, I tend to bunch up words with multiple *ss*'s."

"E-NUN-CI-ATE, my dear boy," said Ethel. "E-NUN-CI-ATE, let it RRR-oll off the tongue, open all the way, that will cure your sloppy speech."

"Thank you, Miss Barrymore, I'll remember that." "See that you do, prrr-oper speech will get you far in life. Perhaps elocution lessons are in order here." I was beginning to sweat furiously, so I was glad that Ken Niles had returned to the stage and had begun to introduce the sketch with Iris, Jack Carson, and Phil Silvers.

Carson and Silvers were playing would-be actors at a casting call and Iris was the receptionist, a role she had played many times.

Iris was sitting behind a desk and filing her nails, musing dreamily. "Ahh, Clark Gable............now there's an ACTOR! So smooth, so suave"—she pronounced it "swav-ee"—"so........so CLARK GABLE! I'd go to see him in anything."

Will I Ever Know

"Even in your pajamas?" quipped Silvers. Big laugh. "Clark Gable," said Carson disgustedly, "what's he got that I couldn't have rearranged?" Bigger laugh.

"Look, you two lugs couldn't act your way out of a paper bag!" said Iris. Another big laugh, some applause, and Carson and Silvers turned to the audience giving us all a dirty look.

"Look, sister," said Carson, "we didn't come here to be disrespected."

"Oh really?" said Iris. "Where do you usually go?" That got another big laugh from the crowd. The skit went on, and when it was over these three pro's got a well-deserved ovation.

Then came the great Charles Laughton doing a scene from King Lear. I was mesmerized as this icon of stage and screen held us captive in the palm of his hand. Every word a masterpiece in itself. Ethel tapped me on the arm and mimed the word "D-I-C-T-I-O-N," pointing at Laughton and nodding her head. I, of course, nodded back.

Then it was time……… time for Frances' encore. Drum roll, Ken Niles the emcee, dramatically announcing, "Now let's welcome back that sweetheart of song, the Dixie Pixie, the ravishing FRANCES LANGFORD!!!!!!!!" Thunderous applause, and a big flourish from the band. Frances took the stage. Was it my imagination or was there a halo above her head? As the applause died down, Frances spoke into the microphone.

"Our job at Command Performance is to be the personal secretaries to all our fighting men. Here is one of the most requested songs." The band then went into a stunning intro. of "You Made Me Love You," as she sang the phrase "gimme gimme gimme what I cry for, you know you've got the brand of kisses that I'd die for, you know you made me love you."

Frances looked right at me as she sang those scorching words. Out of the corner of my eye, I saw that Ethel had seen Frances looking at me as she sang those words. The lorgnette was poised once again as she looked me up and down. I expected a "Harrumph" or something similar, but none came. Just a warm smile.

As Frances finished up the song, she received a standing ovation. So enthusiastic was the ovation that Frances blew kisses all over the auditorium, but there was a wink attached to the one she blew my way.

"She's adorable, and I think you know it, too," whispered Ethel, and she gave me a little wink. I nodded enthusiastically.

The show went on but I kept replaying Frances' performances in my head. "At Last" and "You Made Me Love You" both held tremendous significance for me. 'At Last' meaning that she had found her true love, and 'You Made Me Love You' perhaps alluding to my "dropping" into her life, convincing her who I am and the fulfillment of 'Will I Ever Know'. I hoped they had significance for her also.

The finale was a big ensemble number, with the full cast doing a medley of patriotic songs and Bob Hope doing a narration. With the war just ended, this was just one of many celebrations that had been thrown together quickly. But it came off so smoothly, it was like they had rehearsed for weeks.

I bid farewell to Ethel Barrymore, we shook hands and wished each other well, and I headed for backstage. I had the pass in my hand that Frances had given me, somehow doubting that the burly security guard at the stage door would let me through. I reached the door along with, so it seemed, thousands of other people, all with passes from different stars.

To my surprise as I got to the head of the line, the burly security guard looked at the pass and smiled. "Go right in, sir, Miss Langford is in dressing room 12." So in I went, hotel blazer and all!

What a mob scene! It was if the whole audience had somehow materialized to back stage. I was moved along by the crowd, frantically searching for dressing room 12. My head felt like it was on a revolving turret.

"You look lost, buddy, can I help you?" said a voice to my right. It was Humphrey Bogart. "You...... You..... You're Humphrey Bogart!" I managed to squeak out, remembering too late Ethel Barrymore's stressing, "E-NUN-CI-ATE" and "D-I-C-T-I-O-N."

He gave me that Bogart smile. "Last time I checked I was Humphrey Bogart," he said with a chuckle.

I showed him the backstage pass from Frances and he said, "Oh, you're here to see Doll-face, you lucky stiff. I've been trying to get next to her for years. Dressing room 12, go down this corridor, make a right, and it should be right there on the corner. It's one of the bigger ones. Good luck, chum." Then he gave me that Bogie smile that told me he knew exactly what was up.

I followed Bogie's instructions and they were right on the money. As I turned the corner, there was #12 on the door with "FRANCES LANGFORD" in big letters and a big star right under her name.

At the door I knocked rather timidly; I could hear lots of muffled voices coming from behind the closed door. I knocked louder. The door was answered by a maid, but it wasn't Dora. She was probably staff from the auditorium.

"Chad Henson to see Miss Langford," I almost yelled as I flashed the pass at her. The voices were getting louder with the door open. She had me come in.

This wasn't a dressing room; it was more like a fancy hotel suite with at least three large rooms. There had to be at least fifty people in there, and I did turret-head again to take it all in. From behind me came a crystal-clear voice, "Chad, darling," as Frances threw her arms around me. I replied, "its Chad Henson, remember? Let's not go through the last name thing again."

"Oh you" laughed Frances, "you're worse than Bob Hope."

"Somebody call me?" It was Bob Hope. He said, "Hi'ya, Chad, I just came in here to get away from the crowd in my dressing room, it's the size of a small phone booth. There must be five or six people in there. You know the types—bookies, loan sharks, gangsters, Phil Harris."

"Frances, you were wonderful," I said, "never heard you any better." I gave her a big hug and we kissed lightly.

Bob said, "Yes, you were terrific, sensational, hot, and then some, but listen, Langford. I hate to break this up, but I need to know what you're going to sing on the program tomorrow."

"Oh, you'll never know," said Frances.

Charles Henry

"Now listen, young lady, don't high-hat me, don't let all of this adulation go to your head, it's my show and I need to know."

"That's right," said Frances, "you'll never know."

"Langford, I never thought you'd go high-hat on me, I'm surprised and a little hurt, you know everything goes through me."

"They've got medicine for that now, Bob, maybe you need to see a doctor," joked Frances.

"Now cut that out," said Hope. "What is this, a rejected Abbott and Costello routine?" By now we were all laughing. Bob was picking on Frances, something he loved to do.

"Bob," said Frances, "the title of the song is 'You'll Never Know'."

"And you thought you could keep it from me, that'll teach you, Mother Langford." Then he said to me, "I love to pick on her, she's so.........pickable. You know I refer to her as 'Mother Langford' because she was like a little mother to all of us on the tours, looking out for everybody, while keeping in place her 'hands off policy'." Frances said, "Excuse me a minute, boys, I need to say a few words to Kate Hepburn over there, I'll be right back."

Bob said to me, "That Langford is really something, isn't she? You don't have to say a word, your face says it all. Langford is so savvy, she knows just how much sex to put in without being vulgar, if you know what I mean? Chew on that, Jackson. Excuse me, I think the fuzz are raiding my dressing room, see you tomorrow at the studio." And with that he was gone. I wondered exactly what my face was saying; I think I knew but was afraid to stand in front of a mirror.

Frances came back and queried, "Where's Bob?" "He went back to his dressing room," I said.

"Pardon me, I just had to come over and say a few words." It was the grand voice of Charles Laughton, Shakespearean actor and film star; the man definitely had a way with words. I was completely in awe of Laughton and could barely form a coherent sentence. He was very gracious as he complimented Frances.

Will I Ever Know

"Dear lady," he said in that magnificent speaking voice, "you have taken us to the ethereal spheres with your magnificent voice, which is in every way equal to your legendary beauty." And then he kissed her hand.

"Thank you so much" was Frances reply, and she kissed him on the cheek.

"Ah, my dear, I feel like I've been touched by an angel, smiled upon by the gods, good evening to you both." And he was off.

"Chad, I think you're a bit starstruck," laughed Frances as Charles Laughton made his exit. "Your mouth didn't close the whole time we were talking to Charles."

"I'm sorry, I guess I am, but these are all people I've only seen on screen and they're all g---. I mean, I never thought I'd get to meet them, but for me there is only one star, and that's you," and I kissed her warmly.

Pushing me lightly away, she whispered, "Not here, we'll have plenty of time for that later." Knowing she was right, I suddenly remembered that we were surrounded by many, many witnesses.

As we continued to meet and greet celebrities who were coming and going from Frances' dressing room, I loved the way she was introducing me to these people. It went like this: "I'd like you to meet Chad Henson, an old friend who dropped in unexpectedly." That cracked me up every time, the dropping in, literally, unexpected.

There was to be an after-show party at the Brown Derby for all the members of the cast and "selected" guests. It was "very proper" and very black tie. Frances said there was no problem with my going, tan hotel blazer and all. Then Bob Hope came to my rescue. He had come back to Frances' dressing room because, as he said, "It's lonely in my dressing room."

"Listen, Jackson, why don't you wear my tux, and I'll go with my blue suit that I came in here with? Looking me up and down, we're about the same size."

"Thank you, Mr. Hope, but you don't have to do that."

"Yes I do, Frances is part of my show, you're part of her entourage. I don't want to read in the paper tomorrow that the Bob Hope crew mistook this affair for an early Halloween party," and he winked.

"Thanks, Bob," said Frances.

"Come on, Jackson, let's make the switch."

I followed Bob to his dressing room and changed into his tux. We talked about the show, about how well it went for being just thrown together.

He then started asking some questions about me: where I was from, what I did for a living, general questions which I tried my best to deflect, but not rouse any suspicions.

He didn't mention Frances at all, which was a relief but also a little scary, making me wonder what he knew or what he suspected. As he finished putting on his blue suit I said, "Mr. Hope, now you're going to stand out."

"Relax, my boy, I'm a star, I need to stand out." And we both laughed again. The tux was a little snug but didn't look all that bad.

A button-fly again; oh how I longed for a zipper! The shoes were a bit large but so nice and shiny, much better than the beat-up shoes I had on. Bob looked at the finished product, giving me the twice over.

"Say, Jackson, alright, you're really togged to the bricks!" I wasn't sure what that meant, but I took it as a compliment.

Even though Frances had concocted that story about me being an "old friend who dropped in unexpectedly," it was assumed, hopefully, by Bob Hope and everyone that I was simply an escort for Frances, a prop from central casting, with Jon Hall being away on location. No Hollywood star would ever own up to being at a big shindig with an escort from a movie studio.

"Okay, Jackson, let's roll," said Bob. Frances was waiting outside Bob's dressing room. "See you at the party," said Bob.

"Chad, you look fabulous, you're togged to the bricks, I like a man in a tuxedo." There was that phrase again. Coming from Frances, I knew it had to be a compliment.

"Thank you, I feel a bit like an overweight penguin, but I appreciate Bob lending me his suit."

Frances went over and plucked Iris out of a "serious" discussion with one of the set directors from RKO, and we were off to the "Derby."

Chapter 34
The Brown Derby

The Brown Derby was a restaurant/bar that was physically shaped like a man's derby hat. It was the first restaurant to serve chiffon cake. It was there that the "Cobb salad" was born. It featured hundreds of caricatures of famous celebrities. It was crowded every night, but it was packed this night.

Feeling more comfortable in a tux than I thought was possible, I began rubbernecking again at all the celebrities. We were shown to a ringside table where we could see and be seen.

Phil Silvers was the emcee and he was well suited for it. The future Sgt. Bilko told a few jokes, and Xavier Cugats' orchestra played a terrific version of "Tico Tico."

Someone spotted Frances and started a rhythmic applause as the crowd began to chant "FRANces, FRANces." "I was afraid of this," whispered Frances. "I'd better go sing something."

She walked over to Cugat and whispered something to him. She wanted to sing "Sleigh Ride in July," a new song that she was very fond of. To her delight, the band knew it and began playing the intro. Frances began to sing…….. "I was taken for a sleigh ride in July, O I must have been a set up for a sigh." Ah, that dark creamy voice, like cool water in a babbling brook. Those first two lines are too wonderful for words! Another line is "a balmy summer's eve." Frances was born and raised in Florida, so she does have a twinge of a Southern accent. When she sings the word "balmy," it comes out like "BAH-L-MEH." It's so cute. I listen for that word every time I hear the song.

Well, song over and another standing ovation. People had gotten up and were dancing to "Sleigh Ride." Frances came back to the table and pulled me up for a dance as the band went into "Dancing Cheek to Cheek." Now we were on the dance floor and Frances began to sing the song in a dreamy whisper. This one was just for me. I felt as if my feet weren't touching the floor as she crooned that lovely song into my ear. Frances and I danced several dances. We agreed that we'd talk later; right now just holding each other on the dance floor was enough. Not being much of a dancer, Frances tried teaching me the "cha-cha" and the "rhumba"— without great success, but it was a lot of fun.

After spending a couple of hours at the party, Frances suggested that we leave. She had to prepare for the Hope show. It was going to be another big day. I didn't realize how big. Iris remained at the party, saying she'd catch a ride back to Frances' house. "You two go ahead, there's still a lot more party here," shouted Iris.

Chapter 35
After Party glow

I t was after 1:30 when we got into her car, and as we drove home I began to feel a little melancholy.

Frances said, "Wasn't that a great show and party? A real celebration for the end of the war, with all those stars performing so wonderfully."

"Yes, it was some spectacle."

Then I said, "Frances, don't take this the wrong way, but I……..I don't belong here, here in this world, your world. All those people, loving you, adoring you, prominent people, important people, people that are, well, somebodies. I'm just a nobody from the 21st century. A nobody from the future. You deserve so much better."

Frances pulled the car over to the side. "Now hold on, cowboy," said Frances. "I think you've forgotten our song. 'The moment that I see him I will know him, no matter how impossible it seems.' I haven't been dreaming of some celebrity or rich tycoon or VIP, I've been dreaming of YOU, someone who will give me true love and to whom I can give true love to. Those people are very nice, fun to be with but all of them put together can't come up to what you and I have. That special bond that transcends time and space." I could see tears glistening in her eyes. She never looked more beautiful.

"I'm sorry, sweetheart," I said, "it's just that you are too wonderful for words."

Will I Ever Know

Frances smiled. "That sounds like a cue for another song!" And we leaned into each other for a warm, reassuring kiss. Frances had allayed my fears, all except one: the professor and the Time Machine.

Arriving home, Frances left the car in front for Edward to put away. He was still up! As he passed me I whispered a "thank you" to him and he nodded knowingly. It was good to be "home." I had only been away a short time, but it seemed like eons. Frances and I went into the library.

"Care for a night cap, Chad?" said Frances. "Just some water will be fine, thank you."

Never having been much of a drinker, I had had a couple of highballs at the party, so now I was feeling a little woozy and tired. Frances poured us a couple of glasses of water.

"Some nightcap, huh, Chad?" laughed Frances. "I'm not much of a drinker either."

"Chad, I owe you an apology for what happened." I started to protest but she held a hand up and went on.

"Poor Iris means well, but she's no Sam Spade," continued Frances.

"She needs to work on her spelling too," I said. But Frances wasn't laughing; she was all serious.

"I know that Iris looks out for you."

"Yes, but sometimes she gets carried away," said Frances.

"Say, how did all of this get started anyway, and how did it get resolved?"

"It was all a big misunderstanding," said Frances, and I blame myself for not letting you explain. Iris looked up your name in the L.A. phone book and found a listing for a 'CHAD HANSON.' Not realizing the spelling was wrong, she went into the city to this Chad Hanson's rooming house. Talking to the building superintendent, she found out that Chad Hanson was out on parole for passing bad checks and for fraud. The super said he was working in a grocery store several blocks away and had been missing since the 15th. Iris went to the grocery store and the manager verified everything the superintendent had said. He also told her that Chad Hanson had not been at work since the 14th and had not called or offered any explanation to say what was wrong. Also, he is wanted for questioning in a jewelry robbery where somebody was shot and killed."

"Wow," I said, "Iris must have had a fit."

"She felt as if she had cracked the 'Chad mystery' case wide open. She was convinced you were out to steal my money, or worse. Chad Hanson was in big trouble for violating his parole, and she thought I'd be in trouble for harboring a fugitive. This all happened while we were at the picnic. Remember the way she rushed in?"

"No wonder you were ready to throw me out," I said.

Frances continued, "I was heartbroken. All of my hopes and dreams relating to 'Will I Ever Know' were wrapped up in you. Part of me felt that all my fantasizing about this great love coming to me was just folly. I felt foolish and naïve, but a bigger part of me believed you, wanted to believe you, but now there was proof—so we thought—that you were a fake. I was hurt, angry, and not willing to give you a listen. I..... I just wanted you out, out of my life, out of my heart. It was all too much, especially after the picnic."

"Oh, you poor dear," I said as I grabbed her hand. "I had no idea what was going on."

"I watched the car leave, with you in it as it drove away," continued Frances. "I wanted to rush out of the house, run after it, stop it and bring you back, but I just stood there, frozen."

"Then I guess I fell asleep. I felt like a zombie at the rehearsal for the show, hating the songs I was supposed to sing because they reminded me so of you and what was gone. The next day, I woke up and I was wandering around aimlessly. I went into your room and found the clothes we bought for you hanging in the closet. I ran to them and hugged them, hoping somehow you would be in them, crying again as I realized you were gone. But there was something in the jacket. In the inside pocket was your wallet, I suppose in your haste to leave you forgot it. I opened it up with trembling hands, looking at your things. I pulled out your driver's license with your picture on it and through the tears I read and re-read the information on it. Then it hit me! The license read 'CHAD HENSON.' Iris had been talking about someone whose name sounded like 'CHAD HANSON.' So I called her into the room and had her spell your last name. She kept spelling 'Henson' with an 'A' instead of 'E'. We had to be sure, so we drove into the city to the rooming house and the grocery store. We showed the superintendent of the rooming house and the grocery store manager your picture on the license, and both were very firm that it was not the Chad Hanson they knew. They also verified the spelling, that their guy was HANSON, not HENSON. Then we called Edward back at the house to find out where he'd dropped you off. The rest you know. Oh, here is your wallet." She handed me the wallet, and I was very grateful for my forgetfulness in leaving it behind. Sometimes it helps being absent-minded!

I put my arms around Frances; it was like holding a feather. "Thank goodness for the 'E' in 'HENSON'," I said.

"I think deep down, I knew that wasn't you all the time, it was all such a shock. You would never do anything dishonest."

"Well, I did steal a ride on the professor's Time Machine." We both laughed but there it was again, that cloud on my sunny day. Professor Von Schlaben and the Time Machine. I could be yanked out of here at any moment. I desperately wanted to stay with Frances in 1945. We'd deal with Jon Hall later. I just couldn't let her go.

Frances interrupted my musing by saying, "We'd better get to bed, big day tomorrow, or really today, it's after 2 a.m. I'd also like to drop in on the gang at the set and see how the movie is coming along without me." We both laughed at that, but somehow I didn't want to go back to the movie set because that's where I'd "dropped in."

We went up that beautiful staircase to our rooms, stopping at the door of Frances' room. "Well, goodnight, sweetheart," I said to her and kissed her warmly.

"Listen, Chad," said Frances shyly, "Iris won't be home till dawn or after. In fact, she may crash with someone from the party, Dora and Edward are fast asleep, so we've got the hours to ourselves." She looked at me and smiled that smile. The next sound heard was her bedroom door closing with both of us behind it.

Chapter 36
The Hope Show

We awoke almost simultaneously at 7:30 a.m. Frances snuggled up to me as we hugged and kissed each other awake. "No, no, Chad darling, no time for that now, I want to be at the studio by 11 and it's a long ride."

"I keep telling you it's CHAD HENSON, not HANSON or CHAD DARLING, let's not get mixed up with the names again," laughed I. Frances hit me with a pillow and leaned close and said in a low purring voice, "You'll never be anything but CHAD DARLING to me," as we kissed again. "Now, up up up," said Frances, "no dilly dallying."

"Oh, I'm up," I said devilishly. She hit me with the pillow again.

"You better go to your room and muss the sheets up a bit, make it look like you slept in there."

"I'd rather muss them up with you," I said, grabbing for her. She jumped playfully out of the way. "I think maybe you need a cold shower" was her sly rejoinder.

I went to my room and mussed the bed up, but somehow it looked fake to me. I was exhausted but very happy as I took Frances' advice and took that shower. I hung up Bob's tuxedo and dressed in my 1945 clothes. It was good to get back into them, button-fly and all.

Will I Ever Know

I went in to the dining room and Frances was already there, dressed in a lovely tan suit with matching sleeveless top. For a woman, she was a very fast dresser. I guess it came from having to do so many quick changes in shows and movies. What was it with women and suits in those days? Must have been the "Joan Crawford" influence, I suspected. Her hair flowed beautifully down her back in a golden cascade, still with the "V-for-victory" look.

"Iris isn't home yet," said Frances. "She probably did as I said and stayed with someone from the party. I hope she gets here soon, she needs to go to the studio too." Suddenly I was concerned about Iris. We had started off as antagonists, but knowing how badly she'd felt about the "big misunderstanding," I had come to really like her.

With that, the front door flew open and in came Iris, declaring, "I'm gonna sleep for a week!"

"No no no, young lady, you've got to come to the studio with us, they're thinking of replacing you with Adele Jergens in the movie," cautioned Frances.

Iris took off like a flash for the second floor. Frances laughed. "That will get her going, I just made that up. She and Adele can't stand each other and it seems like they are always up for the same part."

Iris's part in *The Bamboo Blond* was a good one. Lots of dialogue. She certainly didn't want to lose the role.

Adele Jergens was another one of those "B" movie beauties that made a lot of films and did some early TV. A hard worker, she never got the recognition she deserved.

In what seemed like a blink of an eye, Iris was back in the dining room, completely changed, a green suit for her, and crying out, "Coffee, I need coffee............fast!"

Dora was right there with the coffee pot and cup for Iris. Iris had had very little if any sleep, but you'd never know it to look at her. She was ready..............for anything.

"What a party," exclaimed Iris. "I think it's still going on."

"Who brought you home?" asked Frances.

Charles Henry

"A lot of us crashed at Errol Flynn's, I got about two hours sleep. His chauffeur dropped me off here. He had a car full!" laughed Iris.

"Well, let's go, what are we waiting for?" said Iris. "That Jergens dame ain't gonna steal this part from me."

"Relax, Iris, I was only kidding, I wanted to make sure you wouldn't fall asleep on us and make us late."

"Very funny, Blondie," smirked Iris. "Well, here I am anyway."

"It's almost 9," said Frances. "We had better get going. Edward, we'll take the Caddy."

Edward went out to pull the car around. It was another beautiful southern California day. Clear blue sky, wispy clouds. Happy hearts.

We were all set to go out the front door and the phone rang. Frances said, "I'll get it." She picked up the phone.

"Hello, Mina, how are you?" It was Bob Hope's secretary, Mina. He called her "his little mina bird."

"He wants me to what?" exclaimed Frances. "But I haven't sung that song in years. I know, but this is short notice. But…….. Yes, but……….. Very well, I'll see if I can find my copy. Okay, see you later. That Hope," fumed Frances.

"What's wrong?" I asked.

"I was supposed to sing only one song tonight, now Bob wants me to do another, a song I haven't sung in a long time, 'Moonglow'."

She went into the library and began sifting through a mountain of sheet music. Iris and I followed her in.

"That's possibly my favorite record of yours," I said. "It's absolutely perfect. In fact, I would say that's my desert island song, you know, if I were marooned on a desert island, that's the one song I would want with me." Frances wasn't impressed as she continued looking. "Provided you had something to play it on, or would you just spin it around on your finger?" quipped Iris, laughing.

"What, oh yes," said Frances, obviously distracted. "Here it is, cobwebs and all, alright, let's get out of here."

We rushed out the door. The car was waiting and running. We piled in and "heavy-foot Langford" peeled out of the driveway.

Frances began to sing "Moonglow"—a cappella, of course. As she got into that beautiful melody I was transformed; absolutely no one could sing "Moonglow" like Frances. As the beautiful sound filled my whole body, suddenly she stopped.

"Damn," she said, "is that a quarter note or an eighth note? Is that a rest or a pause? Oh dear, Skinnay is just going to have to follow me."

Skinnay Ennis and his band were the featured musicians on Bob Hope's show. Used to accompanying singers, I was sure he would have no trouble staying with Frances in the song.

She repeated and repeated the phrase, "We seem to float right through the air," and I actually felt like we were floating right through the air. Finally I asked, "Don't you like this song? Is that why you haven't sung it very much?"

"I like the song alright, in fact I like it very much, it's just that it has been done so well by so many others, I sort of dropped it from my repertory. I wonder why he chose that song and why he wants to quickly throw it in?"

"Maybe he's gonna do a werewolf sketch," chimed Iris, "and he needs a moon reference."

"That would be just like him," said Frances. "I wonder if Lon Chaney Jr. is on the show tonight?"

"Haven't you rehearsed the show at all?" I asked.

"They've been rehearsing all week. I don't usually rehearse until the afternoon of the show with Skinnay, unless I'm going to be in a sketch or something. I was only supposed to do one song tonight, 'You'll Never Know,' because of the movie shooting and the

USO show. That's why I'm puzzled at him throwing in another song at the last minute. And this particular one."

"Well, I for one am looking forward to it! You're going to be sensational!" "Thank you, dear," said Frances, "but Mr. Hope has some explaining to do!"

"Listen, honey," piped in Iris, "you can do that song or any song in your sleep. Speaking of which, wake me when we get to L.A." Iris closed her eyes for some much-needed shut-eye.

Frances continued to sing and hum "Moonglow" softly the rest of the trip. No argument from me; it sounded heavenly.

We got to RKO studios about 11:10 a.m. As we approached the studio gates, Frances called, "Iris, WAKE UP, we're here."

Iris had slept the whole time. They each showed their studio passes to the guard and Frances said, "Hi'ya, Joe, I'm bringing a guest today, Chad Henson." "Good morning, Miss Langford, here's a guest pass for the gentleman." "Thank you, Joe, take care now."

Since I was with someone from the studio, I didn't have to sign in. Had I been by myself, I would have had to go into the security office, sign in, give the location I was going to, put down the name of the person I was visiting, and then get the visitor's pass. Even though the war was over, security was still pretty tight.

Frances drove over to a huge barn-like building with a sign, "SOUND STAGE 28," on the front. Parking off to the side, we walked up to the door. As I went in I heard a rather loud, "Excuse me" from Iris. "Door, Chad, door, remember a gentleman holds the door open for a lady. . . ladies." "Sorry," I said, "I forgot what era I'm in."

I stepped out and held the door open for the girls. "Now you got it," replied Iris, very satisfied. The three of us chuckled about it.

We were greeted, on the set, by wolf whistles and lots of "Hi, doll," "Hey there," etc. Iris said, "I know those weren't meant for me." Frances greeted everyone and it was clear she was a favorite of the crew.

"Hey, Sam, are they shooting today, is Tony around?" Sam looked like a carpenter or painter. "Hi, Miss Langford, yeah, he's over in the office set with Ralph Edwards, they shot his opening scene over again yesterday."

"Thanks, Sam, this is only a visit, I just want to discuss something with him." "Sure thing, Miss Langford, nice seeing you."

We walked some more and we were on the set. All of the scenes were set up right next to each other: the office, the train station, the night club, Mom's pantry, the mansion in Bucks County, with real fake "woods." The only thing that wasn't set up was the cutout cockpit of the airplane. Everything looked so small, relatively, but it would look different on the big screen. There were Tony Mann and Ralph Edwards on the set of what was Ralph's office in the beginning of the film.

"Hiya, fellows," beamed Frances, "just in for a visit."

"Hello, stranger," said Anthony Mann, the director. "I hear you really wowed them last night at the USO benefit and at the Derby."

"It was a lot of fun," said Frances. "The audience was very kind, at both places."

"It's all over the papers," said Ralph Edwards. "Nice of you to grace us with your presence." And he made a deep bow.

"Oh, how you go on, I'm still the plain simple sweet girl I've always been," she chuckled.

Getting serious, "I don't have much time, at the last minute Bob threw in another song for me to do tonight, so I have to get over to NBC and rehearse with Skinnay. You know I don't like the ending of the movie, it's too dull, Russell walking me into the house and then we all sing around the piano. We can come up with something better than that, can't we?"

Tony said, "We've been tossing around some idea's, how about………….." Then for some strange reason I blurted out, "Why don't you have Frances find her way to the house by herself while Russell is out looking for her? She can make peace with his parents, they can all be singing around the piano, perhaps Russell can trip or something and be all dirty when he gets to the house. He sees that all is well through the window and goes in through the kitchen, sneaking up behind Frances and yanking her through the swinging kitchen door. End of story."

"Who the hell is this guy?" shouted Tony. "And why is he always popping up on my set?" Startled, Frances quickly said, "You remember my old friend, Chad Henson, who dropped in unexpectedly the other day."

"Oh yes, yes," said Tony. "What I want to know is how the hell you knew that that was the ending we had been talking about yesterday?"

I wanted to say, "I've only seen this movie twelve dozen times and I bet I know the dialogue better than you do!" Frances had her head in her hands, while Iris turned her back. Think, Chad, think. This isn't Ethel Barrymore you're dealing with here.

"Oh, I don't know," I stammered, "it just seems like a logical ending, gives it a little pizzazz, or you could................."

"Listen, Tony," chimed in Frances, "it doesn't matter who thought of it, it's a good idea, why don't you have them write some dialogue for it and we'll try it out next week."

"It doesn't really need any dialogue," I said. "It can all be done with juuuuuuuuuuuuuu.............." Frances gave me an elbow in the ribs that literally knocked the wind out of me.

"Dialogue, Tony, dialogue, write some snappy phrases and we'll do it next week, we have to go, bye."

And with that, Frances ushered Iris and me to the exit, leaving Anthony Mann and Ralph Edwards scratching their heads. Tony said to Ralph, "I still have one question, just one little teeny weeny question: who the hell IS that guy?" And they went back to work.

"That was a close call, Chad. Whatever made you say that?" Frances whispered angrily.

"I don't know," I said. "I guess I get so caught up in this whole 1945 Hollywood, YOU thing that I forget that I know the future, I guess I really thought that I'd thought of it. I'm sorry, I'll be more careful."

"Don't worry," said Iris, "Tony's a little on edge because the movie is almost finished. He won't like it and will spend long hours deleting, splicing, etc. The good news is that the kitchen door is not a swinging door but a regular door. You missed that one, dearie, that won't be lost on Tony."

"You're right, Iris," said Frances. "It's not a swinging door, thank God!"

"But what about Ralph Edwards?" I asked.

"I'll take care of him," said Iris. "He has enough trouble remembering his lines, let alone what was said five minutes ago."

"I guess it's alright," said Frances, "but let's just get out of here. Chad, did you remember Bob's tux?"

"Yes, I had Edward put it in the trunk along with the shoes he loaned me."

"Okay, good, we're going to be early getting to NBC, which is fine, gives me all afternoon to go over that song."

"Relax, honey," said Iris, "you got that thing nailed. You're gonna moiderlize it!" "That's what I'm afraid of," laughed Frances.

"Say, what size shoe does Bob Hope take? There was room for at least two more feet in those things. I'm not complaining, that was very nice of him to loan me the shoes and the tux. Took a lot of pressure off. And thank you too, Iris, for getting that hotel guy's blazer."

"Aw, forget it, kiddo, I owed you one, more than one."

The drive to NBC was very peaceful, the three of us chatting away like old friends. I was so glad that Iris had come around. I was very glad to be on her "good" side instead of where I had been previously.

We pulled into the NBC parking lot and walked into the building. Frances and Iris both had ID for NBC and once again Frances greeted the security guard with a smile and friendly "hello."

"Hi, Harry," she said, "great day! This is an old friend of mine, Chad Henson, he'll be here all day with us." Harry scribbled out a temporary pass for me.

Charles Henry

"Mornin', Miss Langford, Miss Adrian, you're both lookin' 'top drawer' today." "We'll take that as a compliment," said Iris.

"Thank you, Harry, you're looking 'top drawer' yourself," winked Frances.

"And good day to you too, sir," I nodded to Harry, thanking him for the pass.

Taking the elevator to the third floor where Bob Hope had his offices, we dropped off the tux and the shoes with the receptionist. At that point Iris left us. She had two shows to do that day—one in the afternoon, and one right after the Hope show. Plus she was in pre-liminary rehearsals for a show next week.

"How do you keep them all straight?" I asked her.

"It's easy, this is radio, remember? We have the script in our hands."

"But what about your mind-set, getting into character, keeping them separate?" "Listen, junior, this ain't Shakespeare, these shows come at us so fast, we ain't got time to think about 'motivation' and character study. The rule in radio is 'show up on time, do your lines, leave.' A simple three-step process, I'll check in with you darlings later." And she was off.

I was sure there was more to it than that, but Iris was a pro and so was Frances; they had the routine down by heart. What Frances didn't have down by heart was "Moonglow," so we set out to find Skinnay Ennis right away. However, the first person we ran into was Bob Hope.

"Hiya, Doll face and Jackson," said Hope. "Listen, Frances, we need to go over your lines for the deli sketch, it's not much since you're doing two songs, we're gonna let you slide for most of the show."

"I can't be thinking about a sketch right now, Bob, I need to find Skinnay and go over that damn song you threw at me at the last minute."

"Whoa, Mother Langford," said Bob, "don't get your horse feathers caught in the saddle, you'll sail right through that old number. Everybody's gonna dig it."

"Sail right through it, my foot! I need more than your wind to 'sail' right through it. The way I sing 'Moonglow,' the tempo needs to be slow and soft and I need huge amounts of air to give me the support I need so that I don't crack any of the notes."

"We'll get you an oxygen tank, put it right by the microphone" was Bob's reply with an attempt at humor.

"I don't need an oxygen tank, I need Skinnay Ennis and the band. We need to work on where I can break. That song is like one long sustained note, I need to break and breathe and make it look like I didn't break and breathe."

"Look, sweetie, Skin' isn't here yet but he will be here shortly, so cool your heels." "Why that song, Bob?" asked Frances.

"Skinny and I were listening to your record of it, and we felt it would fit perfectly into the sketch with Jack Carson. The one where he is in the park at night with the girl."

"But you know I haven't sung that song in over five years, it's not an easy one to do even though it sounds simple."

"You worry too much, doll, you'll be great as you always are. Most of the band is in the rehearsal room if you want to go and get started with them."

"Yes, I think I'll do that," said Frances, "but Skinny better hurry up and get here."

Bob kissed her lightly on the cheek and said, "Go git 'em, tiger!"

Then he turned to me, "That tuxedo worked out okay for you, didn't it, Jackson?" "Sure did, Bob, and thank you again. I left it with your receptionist."

"That's fine, Jackson, glad to do it." He went down the hall and went into a room marked "Writers."

"Come on, Chad, let's find the band," said Frances, clutching her copy of "Moonglow."

We came to a large door marked "Rehearsal Room." As we entered, we were met by a chorus of wolf whistles and shouted greetings. This seemed to relax Frances as she smiled and said, "Hiya, fella's, good to see all of you."

Charles Henry

She went to the bandstand and asked the group if they were familiar with "Moonglow." One of the trombone players piped up, "No, but you can show me tonight if you want." They all laughed and howled. Frances said, "No, silly, the SONG!" To a man they all shouted, "NO!" Frances turned to me and said, "See what I have to put up with?"

"Fella's, this is Chad Henson, an old friend who dropped in unexpectedly"; she had that line down perfectly. There was a chorus of "Hi's," "How are ya's," etc. Then the door opened and the man of the hour, Skinnay Ennis, walked in.

Meanwhile................ somewhere in the sky not too far from Los Angeles, Jon Hall was returning home. He was seated on the plane next to his publicist, Jay Morino.

"Ah, good to be going home, it's been a long six weeks," said Jon.

"The preliminary reports look good on the background scenes," said Jay. "I think we got a winner on our hands, guy."

Jon had been on location in South Africa, shooting background shots and scenes of ruins for the epic swashbuckler CORTEZ RULER of the DESERT for Universal. Set in 14th-century Spain, the studio had high hopes for this one. Jon Hall was famous for this type of role. However, it got shelved a quarter of the way into production, never to be finished.

Jon was in a very good mood. "I think I'll go right to NBC and catch Frances on the Hope show, I'll ride back home with her."

"Listen," said Jay, "when's the last time you wrote to her? I bet you didn't write at all during the six weeks you've been gone."

"I've been busy, Jay, with *Ruler of the Desert*, Frances understands, she's super busy too. What with the Hope show, her movies, and USO involvement, we never get to see each other."

"Just the same, that's no excuse, she wrote you several long letters."

"I'm not much of a letter writer, she understands that."

"I sure hope so, Jon, wives can be funny about stuff like that."

Will I Ever Know

"She likes surprises, so I'm sure she'll like me showing up at the broadcast tonight."

"Did you see the paper, Jon? Frannie was quite a big hit last night at the USO show and the party at the Brown Derby. Look, here she is at the USO show and over on page 11, there she is at the Derby."

"Say, Jon," said Jay, "who's with Frances in these pictures? Nobody I recognize."

It was me caught by several photographers, and there we were spread out all over the L.A. papers.

"Probably some guy from Central Casting, providing an escort for Frances." Jon put his head back and fell asleep, very contented.

At NBC, Frances was doing wonderfully with "Moonglow" and so were Skinnay Ennis and the band. And I got to see and hear everything. "That wasn't bad," said Frances. "Skinnay, you're the best!"

"I been listening to your record all week, Sunshine, we'll be hep and you'll be smooth."

"Skinnay, this is an old friend, Chad, he'll be watching the show tonight."

"FAB-O," he said as he put out his hand, "slip me some skin, Chadzford," which was musicians' talk for "let's shake hands."

Skinnay Ennis had one of the most popular bands in the Los Angeles area at the time. They were also nationally known because of their many radio broadcasts. He was the music director of the Bob Hope show and was the butt of many of Bob's jokes. He appeared in quite a few of the comedy sketches on the show.

"Why don't you cats grab some grub before the show? I gotta get with the Big Boss man for awhile and make sure everything is all reet." And Skinnay went off down the hall.

"That's a good idea," said Frances. "Let's just go down to the cafeteria for a quick bite, I don't want anything big, we'll have a good meal after the show."

"Fine with me," I said, "just a sandwich or something will be fine."

Charles Henry

It was a typical cafeteria, nothing fancy, but with pictures of a lot of NBC radio stars of the period on the walls. We both had grilled cheese sandwiches and Cokes. As we got settled at a table, Frances said seriously, "Chad, what are we going to do? We're in pretty deep." I could hear the anxiety in her voice. "I don't know how much longer I can keep introducing you as 'an old friend who just dropped in unexpectedly'."

"Sweetheart, I want to marry you!" I blurted out. "I love you, you're the fulfillment of everything, the fulfillment of 'Will I Ever Know'."

"Chad, be serious," she whispered. "I'm a married woman, what do I do about that?" "One word…….. 'divorce'."

"I know, darling, but what about Jon? We haven't given a thought about him, what he'll do, how it will affect him."

"I'm divorced," I said. "It's not pretty, someone always gets hurt, but people make mistakes, and sometimes divorce is the only way to correct mistakes. It looks like you and Jon haven't been close for a long time. You each have your own careers and you both travel a lot. With me, I'll be with you all the time. I have no agenda here. My only goal is to spend every second with you. Remember the words to the song, 'no matter how impossible it seems'."

Frances looked away, and I could see she was unsettled. Then she looked me straight in the eye. "I love you too, Chad, more than you'll ever know. I can't bear the thought of not being with you. You are serious, aren't you, about marriage, I mean?"

"Oh sweetheart, YES, YES, that's the reason I'm here, the power of love brought me here, even though this whole thing seems crazy, the fact that technically I won't be born for 30 years, that we are literally from different worlds, none of that matters. We both received a sign. The sign was the song. Talk about two people having 'their song.' 'Will I Ever Know' is truly our song, our sign, the sign that led us to each other. I won't let you go!"

"Oh, Chad, I love you! I really do! I knew it the moment you 'dropped in' and I looked into your eyes. We have to be strong, courageous, and be firm in our convictions. Jon will understand, he has to understand, you know he was married before?"

I knew he was married, before he married Frances, to an actress who was about eight years older than he was. What I didn't tell Frances, although it was on the tip of my tongue, was that after Frances and Jon divorced in 1955, ten years from now, Jon would re-marry the woman he'd divorced to marry Frances.

A thought struck me. If Frances divorced Jon in 1945 and married me, that would change history. The professor's words echoed in my head: "My boy, changing history could turn the cosmos into CHAOS!" We would be rewriting history. But how could the early divorce of two movie stars, ten years before it happened in history, alter the events of the world? What if we had children? What would happen in 1973 when I was supposed to be born? Would I be a sixty-year-old infant?

"Darling, what is it? You look like you're a million miles away," said Frances. "Uh……….. oh, it's nothing," I said, coming back to the reality of 1945. "I guess I kind of zoned out."

"What?" said Frances. "I just get lost in your eyes." Frances looked away. "Oh you, you're too much," she laughed.

"We're going to make it," she said. "This was meant to be!" I gloried in her resolve and I felt confident once again.

The plane was making its descent. "Home at last," said Jon. "I'm tired, but I'm going over to the Hope show anyway. Then it will be time for a long period of peace and quiet. Frances should be through with her movie in a couple of weeks and we can spend endless days at home, in the pool, get to know each other yet again."

"Sounds nice," said Jay. "There are millions of guys who would love to spend some quiet time at home with FRANCES LANGFORD!" They both chuckled warmly.

Arriving at the airport, Jon and Jay got their luggage and went out to the cabstand. "Where are you headed, Jay?" asked Jon.

"I'm going home…to sleep," he said. "My wife knows the routine. Carol will have a martini ready, and then it's beddy-bye Jay."

"Me too," said Jon, "after the Bob Hope show broadcast. I wonder what she'll be singing tonight. I'll find out soon." They each got a cab; Jay headed for the L.A. suburbs, Jon for downtown and NBC.

Charles Henry

The show was ready to start. I was positioned, by Frances, strategically in the wings' stage right where I could see and hear everything without being in the way. After a brief monologue, Bob went on to introduce Frances. "And now here is that beautiful young lady who stood Hollywood on its ear last night at the big Victory USO benefit, MISS FRANCES LANGFORD!"

Frances got a wonderful welcome from the studio audience. She approached the microphone and said, "Good evening to all of you, here's one of my favorite songs, I'm sure you all know it, 'Moonglow'." There were some ooo's and ahhh's from the studio audience as Skinnay Ennis and the band began the soft intro.

Frances was transformed as she half whispered the opening lines. Soft yet clear and strong, she took us under her spell. She hung the words "We seem to float right through the air" literally in the air, hauntingly beautiful, the orchestra in perfect, soft harmony with her. She seemed not to take a breath through the whole thing. With the finishing words, "I'll always remember, that Moonglow gave me you, that Moonglow gave me you," she looked my way and gave me a soft smile. I was in heaven! She held that last "you," making it gradually softer and softer until it disappeared into thin air.

The song was over and there was silence. I wondered what was going on and then the audience, as if it had just awakened from a trance, erupted into thunderous applause that just wouldn't stop.

They were due for a commercial. In those days, the commercials were done live right on the show, so they had to wait for the applause to die down before Ken Niles could start the toothpaste commercial.

Frances came offstage and gave me a big hug as all the crew came over to congratulate her. She didn't say a word, but looked at me with what a song of the future would call "the Look of Love." Then she went off to her dressing room.

Bob Hope came over and whispered, "How 'bout that, Jackson? Isn't she something? Don't say a word, it's written all over your face!" He gave me a wink. The director tapped him on the shoulder and they went off to confer for a moment.

All of a sudden, I felt a tap on MY shoulder. I turned around. It was Jon Hall. "Excuse me," he said, "has Frances Langford done her number yet?"

Will I Ever Know

Flabbergasted, I managed to stammer, "Uh………..uh……………uh, she ju- just finished but she's going to do another one."

"Oh, great," said Jon. "Oh well, at least I'll get to hear one of them. Traffic from the airport was terrible. By the way, I'm Jon Hall, Frances' husband." He shook my hand. "Chad Henson," I said. "I'm just here watching the show."

So there he was, Jon Hall, my boyhood hero from reruns of his very successful TV show *Ramar of the Jungle*. The idol of every eight-year-old boy and girl. We used to act out his adventures in darkest Africa and India. Now he was my rival.

"Jon, glad you could make it," said the director. "You just missed Frances in a beautiful rendition of 'Moonglow'."

"Yes, I know," he replied, "but this gentlemen tells me she has another number." "That's right, she's going to do 'You'll Never Know' in a few minutes."

Bob and Jerry Colonna were doing a very funny bit; the audience was in stitches as they were recalling some funny moments from their USO tours. They were actually cracking each other up.

"Mind if I stand here and watch?" said Jon Hall. "I don't want to bother Frances in her dressing room, there's probably not room for anyone or anything else in there," quipped Jon, looking at both the director and me. Looking at me intensely he said, "Are you in the show……. it's Chad, isn't it? Are you an actor?"

Oh brother, he was talking to me! I was beginning to sweat. "Why, no… no, uh, I'm just here watching the show, guest of a friend."

"Oh, I see," said Jon. "Hope puts on a good show."

"Yes he does." I couldn't think of anything else to say.

The sketch was over; time for another commercial. Bob Hope came over to the wings. "JON," he exclaimed, "welcome home, fella!" and they gave each other a big hug, as the stage manager gave Bob an emphatic "SHUSH!"

"How did the shooting go?" whispered Bob, realizing his greeting might have been loud enough to go out over the air. "When did you get back?"

"I just got back, came here right from the airport," whispered Jon. "I'm really excited about this picture. They're thinking about doing it in color."

"Those folks at Universal, what will they think of next? I'll have to remind them that movies can be made in color," joked Bob. "I have one coming up next year. For once I'd like to see my ruddy complexion on the big screen."

"Just be firm, Bob," chided Jon. "Tell them its color or nothing for your next picture." "Great, just what the movie public is waiting for, 96 minutes of nothing." Jon laughed, I managed a faint laugh. I was beginning to feel a little funny. Must be nerves, I thought, standing so close to Jon Hall.

It was Frances' time to sing again. I could see her coming from the dressing room. Jon turned. "Darling, there you are," he whispered. Frances face fell like a piano being dropped from the roof of a building.

"Jon, what are you doing here?"

"Well, that's some greeting," said Jon. "I just got in and I came right over here from the airport." He held her and was set to give her a kiss, but she turned her head so the kiss landed on her cheek.

"I've got to go on now, please excuse me," she said as she pulled away and went toward the stage. Jon looked puzzled. I just looked. Bob was all set for the intro.

"And now here she is back for an encore, the little lady who traveled so much entertaining the troops, she actually became part of the standard equipment, the Florida thrush herself, FRANCES LANGFORD, right here!"

Frances said, "Now that I'm home from all those wonderful tours, I can still remember the faces of all those brave fighting men and women. What I've been doing lately is trying to catch up on the latest songs, here's one I think you'll all like, 'You'll Never Know'."

I was beginning to feel worse, a little like I was here but I wasn't here, all I could think of was the professor................

Will I Ever Know

Back in the lab, Professor Von Schlaben was working furiously, going over his notes. He typed in a rather long code and hit the ENTER button………………………

Frances seemed to get more intense as she sang the song in her typical dreamy style. The warm, dark contralto mixing with the honeyed pianissimos. She owned the song and the audience knew it. Suddenly I stepped back a few steps, as it felt as if I were being punched in the gut. No one seemed to notice, and then I was fadiiiiiiiiiiiiiiiiiiiiiiiiiiiiiiiii-ing. "NO, No," I shouted, but no sound came out of my mouth. The stage was getting farther away. Frances looked over and saw it too. We both knew what was happening. I was being pulled out of 1945………. Frances, panic and fear written all over her face…………managed the last lines "If there's some other way to prove that I love you, I swear I don't know how, you'll never know. . . if you don't know NNowwww!!!" As she sang "now," it cracked and she fell into hysterical sobbing, running offstage yelling, "CHAD CHAD COME BACK! NO NO NO NO NO NO!!!!!!!!!!!" and she collapsed, fainting. Jon Hall looked at Bob, Bob ran out onstage quickly, the audience buzzing.

Skinnay Ennis looked dazed. Jon Hall rushed over to Frances, trying to revive her. "Frances, Frances, what's wrong?" cried Jon. "What's the matter?"

Bob was onstage, very nervously trying to ad-lib. "Relax, folks, relax, all part of the show, all part of the show, Frances is fine," he said as he furtively looked over to the wings at the crowd that was gathered around Frances' fallen form.

"How about that Langford, isn't she something? When we were on tour, I'd come out and do a little tap dance or something, in the terrible hot sun and heat, mind you. Frances was great, I'm not going to say she was a scene stealer, but next time I think I'll wear a two-piece sun suit too!!!" That broke the tension; the audience laughed, and Bob closed the show. Skinnay played the theme song and it was over. Bob rushed over to the wings. "Is she alright?" he said.

"Chad, oh Chad, where are you, don't leave me, don't leave me, oh Chad," and she was out again.

"Where's that doctor?" yelled Jon. "She's delirious."

The calling of my name was not lost on Bob Hope. He said, "Water, get her some water."

Part IV
1915 & 1945

Chapter 37
I Arrive In 1915/ Frances' Condition

OOOOOOOOOO, I was drifting again, drifting in what seemed like an ethereal fog. Suddenly I plopped down in front of a rather large house on a tree-lined street. The weather was warm. Children were riding bicycles and playing ball.

"Are you all right, old man? You took quite a tumble there."

I looked up and a man was standing over me, about my age. I was trying to figure out where I was now. He was dressed in a bow tie and striped shirt, with a handlebar mustache, and his shiny hair parted down the middle. He looked like he'd just stepped out of a barbershop quartet. The children were dressed in knickers, short coats, and jeff caps.

Wherever I was, I knew it wasn't 1945, my 1945 clothes looking really out of place. "I'm okay," I said, "must have tripped over something, I'm very clumsy." I was starting to get good at explaining my unexpected appearances.

Trying to think of something to say, I said, "I'm looking for a hotel, could you tell me if there are any around here?" Wherever I was, I needed to find a place to stay where I could hash out all that had just happened and try to figure things out.

"Sorry, no hotels close by." A horse and buggy went past us; hmm, must be early 20th century. "But there is a rooming house around the corner, 648, Mrs. Shelby rents rooms. Tell her Dolph Terwiliger sent you."

Charles Henry

"Thank you," I said, "much obliged." I went around the corner and there was a neat, white clapboard, three-story house with a small sign out front that said "Rooms."

I knocked on the door and waited. A little wizened lady answered the door. She was wearing very thick glasses.

"Hello, I'm inquiring about a room, Dolph Terwiliger sent me over," I said.

"Come right in, I'm Agnes Shelby. I have a second-floor rear room and a smaller third floor front."

"I'd like to look at the second floor room, please."

"Alright, follow me, it's a nice clean room, gets lots of fresh air, bathroom down the hall. She unlocked the door and we went in. The room wasn't fancy but it would do. Not like Palm Springs. There was a single bed in the middle of the room, with a chest of drawers and a pitcher for water. A nice view from the window, plenty of fresh, clean air coming in.

"Three dollars a week.....................in advance, young man." I pulled out three dollars; I now had some 1945 money but I didn't know if it would be good here, wherever I was. I decided to be daring. Mrs. Shelby obviously had poor eyesight. I gave her the three dollars, and she looked at them closely but just put them in her apron pocket. That was a relief. Maybe I could ask her to change a ten or twenty later; that way I would have the coin of the realm.

"Dinner's at 6:30P, breakfast at 7A. You're on your own for lunch, and no women, if you get my drift."

"Loud and clear, Mrs. Shelby, I have no one anyway," as my voice broke a little. She softened a bit as a look of sympathy crossed her face. "Alright then, let me know if you need anything." "Thank you," I said.

I needed to get a newspaper to find out what year it was. I freshened up and headed out, stopping Mrs. Shelby to find out where I could get a paper.

"I take it you're new in town, right?" "Yes, I just arrived"—literally, I thought.

Will I Ever Know

"Go down to the corner," she said and pointed. "Turn right, there's a soda shop four blocks down on your right. They sell papers there."

"Thank you, Mrs. Shelby," as I petted her cat. "What's his name?"

"Not a him, it's a her, her name is Peaches."

The cat seemed to like me as I picked her up. She was purring like a motorboat. Peaches was a beautiful tabby, and apparently very affectionate.

"She may find her way into your room, just toss her out."

"I won't mind, I love cats," I replied, "but you said no women." We both laughed. "We'll make an exception for Peaches."

Mrs. Shelby seemed like a nice lady; I just hoped she wasn't a nosey one. Putting Peaches down, I went off to the soda shop. Mrs. Shelby changed a ten-dollar bill for me so I had some real 1915 money.

This town seemed like a nice quiet place. Several people said "hello" to me on the way. I came to a quaint little shop festooned with balloons. I went in and picked up a paper. The masthead read "Lakeland Sentinel" and the date was Sept 17, 1915. So that's where I was, someplace called Lakeland and it was 1915. I sat on a stool with my paper.

The soda jerk came over. "What can I get you?"

"Vanilla ice cream soda, and make it a double." I was feeling so low I needed to lose myself in a real ice cream soda. So low that I felt like I could crawl under a snake with a top hat on. But where could I find a snake wearing a top hat?

"Hey buddy, you okay? You look like you lost your best friend."

"I think I might just have, I think I might just have," as I drowned my sorrows in a double vanilla.

The doctor arrived and administered some smelling salts to Frances. After she came around, she looked in every direction, crying, "Find him, you have to find him!"

Charles Henry

"Who?" asked Jon. "Frannie, what are you talking about? Who do we have to find?" Frances, upon recognizing Jon, got quiet.

"You'll be alright, Miss Langford," said the doctor. "All you need is some rest. You've been a very busy lady, USO tours, big benefit, party, the show tonight. Jon, she's in your care. Make sure she gets some rest."

"You're the doctor. Come on, Frannie, let's go home and get you to bed."

"No, no," said Frances, as she stammered, "gotta find him, gotta find him fast."

"Frances, we're going home, the doctor gave me something to give you that will make you sleep."

Again Frances resisted. "No, no, don't you understand, I must find him."

Someone brought out a chair and they managed to get Frances into a sitting position.

Iris came hurrying over; she had heard about the commotion. "Come on, honey, get up and we'll get you home, I'll come with you."

"Thank you," said Jon, "that will be a big help, nice of you to come." "Yeah, let's get this bad baby home." She made the "shush" sign to Frances.

I started to walk back to Mrs. Shelby's, now full of vanilla ice cream sodas, the newspaper firmly under my arm.

I'd had three doubles altogether, so I was feeling just a bit of discomfort. Coming from the other direction, a young mother was wheeling a stroller with a cute little girl in pink. I started to smile, but then the toddler let out a shriek and began sobbing and trying to get out of the stroller.

Oh boy, I thought, just what I need: a screaming kid.

The mother, embarrassed, quickly went by. Even in the distance, I could hear her wailing. What a pair of lungs on that kid, I thought.

Will I Ever Know

Getting back to the rooming house, I found it empty so I went up to my room. There, perched on the bed, was Peaches, with a "Do not disturb" look on her face. There was a small chair next to the bed, so I settled down and began to use Peaches as a sounding board.

I ruminated on how cruel it had been to yank me out of 1945. Frances and I had big plans, we were going to be married, now what? I suppose I'll rot here in 1915. This is where I'll probably get stuck. The professor will type in a code on the Time Machine, and the thing will blow up in his face and that will be that.

"Well, Peaches," I said, "I guess it's back to the want ads. Let's see if they need any computer programmers here in 1915." Peaches looked at me as if I were giving the Gettysburg Address. What was Frances doing? How was she doing? Did she tell Jon anything or everything?

Chapter 38
I Finally Get A Job/ Frances At Home

Back at the house, they got Frances into bed. Iris had given her a sedative, and she was sleeping.

"Iris, do you have any idea what's going on here? Who is this 'Chad' that Fran keeps talking about? And why is he gone, and where did he go?"

"Jon, there's time later for questions, she's resting, and you must be exhausted, and I'm frankly pooped myself. Let's talk in the morning."

I slept fitfully that night—strange bed, strange environment, I suppose. I had circled a couple of jobs to explore. Both were in retail sales. I prayed they wouldn't ask for references, but I had dreamed up a fictitious job at the *Philadelphia Evening Bulletin* newspaper just in case.

Breakfast was good. Mrs. Shelby proved to be a good cook. Good old-fashioned scrambled eggs and bacon, and good coffee. There were two other roomers. A quiet middle-aged woman, Minerva, and a 60ish-looking man, Lucius. After introductions all around, we ate in silence, Minerva never looking up once. Lucius had his head buried in the racing form. Mrs. Shelby hovered around, bringing more food as the need arose, chirping about the weather, politics, her back.

Will I Ever Know

Peaches made the rounds to each of us, getting a small slice of bacon from me, and then demanding more and making her wants known. Mrs. Shelby banished Peaches from the kitchen after realizing she was paying a lot of attention to me, and seeing me slip her two more small pieces of bacon.

Breakfast over, I asked Mrs. Shelby where Ralph's Emporium was located.

"Go to the end of the block, turn left, it's about three blocks down Main Street at the corner of Spruce. It's a nice place, they have everything from soup to nuts."

"They have a 'help wanted' ad in the paper," I told her, "thought I'd give it a try." "You tell Ralph Finney that Agnes Shelby sent you, and that you're staying here. That should be enough, you need to get a job if you're going to stay here any length of time," declared Mrs. Shelby.

I wildly hoped that Ralph would dispense with the reference thing. Obviously, he and Mrs. Shelby were well acquainted.

It was a beautiful morning, hot but not as hot it would be a little later. I was glad that everything in Lakeland seemed to be in decent walking distance.

Under other circumstances, Lakeland would be a nice town to make home, but I couldn't get Frances out of my mind. She was all I could think about. How was she? What was she doing? What was Jon Hall doing? I hoped I could concentrate on the interview. If I was going to stay here, and keep my room, I needed a job, badly. I couldn't count on Mrs. Shelby taking my 1945 money forever. Plus, there wasn't that much of it. Thank God, though, for Edward's hundred dollars!

Approaching me on the sidewalk was a woman pushing a stroller. As she approached, I recognized her from the soda shop. The baby in the coach was beautiful, and as they got closer, the little girl was looking at me very intently. When I smiled, the mother looked away, but the little girl gave me the sweetest smile, and as they passed she turned around in the stroller and kept looking at me. Now mind you, I don't have anything against babies, but I've never been much of a "baby guy." I have an uneasy truce with children: I don't bother them, they don't bother me, but I was rather taken by the charm of this little one. But then she started to cry and carry on again just like before, screaming, it seemed, right at me. I hastened on.

Charles Henry

Proceeding to Ralph's, I came across a fairly large store with a big sign overhead in very Victorian lettering: "RALPH'S EMPORIUM" "EVERYTHING FROM SOUP TO NUTS," 1915's answer to Value Barn. This must be the place, I thought. Well, here goes!

It was mid-morning, and Frances began to slowly wake up. She had been heavily sedated. Jon and Iris were at her bedside. "What time is it?" she whispered. "Where am I?"

"You're home, darling," said Jon, "how do you feel?" "Where's Ch…" "Where's who?" queried Jon.

"Ah, honey, how about some tea and toast?" piped in Iris. "I brung you some."

"What happened?" whispered Frances.

"You fainted last night after the Hope show," said Jon, "and you kept calling out some-one's name, a Ch…………."

"Alright, dearie, drink some of this, you'll feel better, and eat some toast." "I don't want anything, I just want CH…………" "Don't try to talk, honey," Iris interrupted. "Save your strength, you need to rest."

A desperate Iris was trying to deflect the mention of my name by both Frances and Jon. It was like trying to play a game of tennis by yourself, working both sides of the net.

"Will SOMEBODY please tell me who this person is that she is looking for? I have a right to know, something very strange is going on here."

Frances was very restless. Iris looked at both of them and said, "Jon, let's go downstairs and talk, I'll tell you what I know, but please just let her rest, she's in no condition to be grilled right now."

"Grilled? Who's grilling her? I just want to know………………"

"Jon, please, downstairs, NOW." Iris could be very insistent.

"Alright," said Jon, "it looks like that's the only way I'm going to get any answers."

Will I Ever Know

I went into Ralph's Emporium and a little bell tinkled above the doorway. Inside, it was just like some of those museums you see out west. A general store that did have EVERYTHING. One huge room, with all sorts of clothing, food, and hardware all neatly divided, as well as books and office materials. Two things I didn't see were soup and nuts, but I'm sure they were there.

A spry, elderly man came from the curtained back room, wire spectacles on his nose, a striped shirt, vest, and garters on his sleeves. Just like those wax figures at those museums I mentioned. This must be Ralph.

"What can I do fer ya? Name's Ralph Finney."

"Good morning, sir, my name is Chad Henson, I'm staying at Agnes Shelby's rooming house, she sent me over."

"Well, what does she want? This ain't her ordering day," said Ralph.

"No, no," I said, "I saw your 'help wanted' ad in the paper. I'm here to apply for the job."

"Oh, oh," said Ralph, "well if Agnes Shelby sent you over, you're hired. That woman's got a ken for people. Here's an apron, you can get started." This seemed too easy.

"Don't I have to fill out an application or something?" I asked. Shut up, Chad! the voice in my head screamed.

"Naw, don't bother with them things, waste a time, clutter up ma desk. Oh, the pay is $12.50 a week, that's good for these here parts, and you get a 10% employee's discount on all things. I'll give you a credit account of $20." He looked me up and down. "Looks like you need some decent clothes, where'd ya come from?"

I had forgotten my 1945 outfit. "Why, uh….. I was with a traveling circus, they went belly up, these were the most decent clothes I could muster," I replied nervously. "Yep, uh huh, carny folk, can't trust most of 'em."

"Well, the job ain't hard, give 'em what they want, try to give 'em some of what they don't want. We ain't got it, tell 'em we'll git it. Sweep the floor, keep the stock on the shelves, check the inventory, if we're low, order more, if we got plenty, don't order more. I'm here all the time, doin' just what you're a doin', so any questions just ask. Be here at

Charles Henry

7 a.m. on the dot to get ready to open. We open at 9, close at 6 p.m. on the dot. Take a lunch around 12 or when we ain't busy, half an hour, plenty a time for chow. Six days a week, whatcha do on the seventh is your business." Having had my duties spelled out, I was ready for work.

My first task, I figured, was to give the floor a good sweeping since there were no customers at the moment. This seemed to impress Ralph.

"That's always good to do when ya ain't busy. Ain't busy, sweep, that's ma motto. Simeon Barnes' boy, Jepthah, had the job before ya. Good boy, bright boy. Off to one of them 'colleges' now. Head's gonna be stuffed with all that 'fancy book learnin,' probly come back and run his father's farm. All that 'fancy book learnin' a runnin' around in his brain, give him somethin' to think about when he's a plowin' the field! Ain't that right, bub?" With that, Ralph broke into laughter that wouldn't stop. I laughed with him.

The hours were long, the pay small, but then again this was 1915. I used my store credit to get some clothes; I think that was what Ralph was hinting at. Still, it was nice of him to do it. I got a suit with an extra pair of pants, two shirts, one blue-and-white stripes, the other red-and-white stripes. Striped shirts seemed to be the "in" thing, at least in Lakeland. I also got a high pair of shoes, to hide my plaid socks, and another pair of socks and some underwear. That used up my $20 credit and then some. I threw in a $10 bill from my "Edward" money and buried it in the cash register with some other tens, hoping Ralph wouldn't notice.

My breakfast and dinner partners continued in their silence, and outside of Mrs. Shelby, the friendliest sort in the rooming house was Peaches, who would be found in my room almost every morning when I woke up.

Chapter 39
Rose Fowkes/ Jon Demands Answers

O n Saturday morning around 10:30, in walked a rather attractive, youngish woman. I was behind the counter. She said, "Good morning, sir, my name is Rose Fowkes."

"Alright, Iris, let's have it, and I mean all of it," said a very angry Jon Hall. "Who is this Chad Whatever, and what has he got to do with Frances? There was a Chad something or other in the wings next to me last night at the show."

Iris began, "A few days ago, on the set, this guy showed up, said he was a big fan of Frances. He had a scrapbook full of Frances' photos and clippings. He seemed harmless. Frances seemed to take a liking to him, or rather maybe felt sorry for him. She talked to him awhile and she invited him to the USO benefit and the broadcast of Bob Hope's show the following night. We ALL went together, the THREE of us. That's it, that's all I know." Iris conveniently left out the parts about my staying at the house, the picnic, and the misunderstanding.

"That's all you know. The total. Everything. That doesn't explain why the film's shooting was suspended for a week, that doesn't explain why some strange men's clothing was found in OUR guest room," said Jon, his voice rising to a fever pitch. "And that doesn't explain why Frances is near a nervous breakdown, crying out for this…this Chad person and won't even talk to me."

Charles Henry

"Jon, it's not what you think," said Iris. "Look, he's gone, why not just let it go?"

"I'm not letting it go, I'm NOT letting it go," stormed Jon. "I go away for six weeks, working my ass off on what could be the biggest movie of my career, I come home to find my wife in a state of hysteria over some 'phantom' man. I want answers, I demand answers, I have a right to answers and since you won't tell me, I'm going to make her tell me!"

Jon stormed out of the library, heading up the stairs to their room.

"Jon, please," called Iris, "let her rest, she's been through enough!" "She's going to tell me what I want to know or else!" called Jon from the top of the stairs.

Finding the door locked, he called out, "FRANCES............FRANCES........ OPEN THIS DOOR," as he pounded vigorously.

"Go AWAY!" came the muffled reply from behind the door. Then there was a tremendous crash and the sound of wood separating from wood. He had broken the door open. Frances was curled up in the bed. Jon stood at the doorway.

"You're going to tell me what I want to know. Everything about CHAD!"

"You're new here, aren't you?" said Rose.

"Yes, my name is Chad Henson, I started here a few days ago."

"Hmm," she said, "you're older than Jepthah."

"I never met Jepthah, I assume he's still a teenager, I'm 34."

"34, how nice," mused Rose. "I'm the school teacher, I've been teaching here in Lakeland for three years, I'm 27. Are you going to be staying here in Lakeland permanently, Mr. Henson?"

Not sure if I was going to be anywhere "permanently," what with Prof. Von Schlaban being button-happy back in the present, I said, "Not rightly sure at the present time, ma'am."

Will I Ever Know

Hoping that would put an end to that and trying to adapt to the local speech pattern, I started rearranging things on the counter.

"Well, I hope you do," said Rose. "We need some more mature, handsome men in Lakeland. Good day to you, sir, very nice to make your acquaintance."

"And good day to you too, ma'am," and she walked out the door without buying anything. Oh, great, I thought. I don't need any new romantic entanglements; my only thoughts were how I could get back to Frances.

Ralph came out of the back room. "Was that Rose Fowkes?"

"Yes it was, or that's who she said it was," I said.

"Didn't she buy anything?"

"No, she just walked in, introduced herself, and left."

Ralph said, "I guess the chatterbox chain is at work. A new, eligible man in town, word gets around.........fast. I assume you are 'eligible'. Not wanting to get into the divorce thing, because in 1915 I might be fired for being divorced and I certainly didn't want to get into the Frances thing, I just said, "Yes, I'm single."

"Lemme tell ya, bub, the whole entire female population of Lakeland are flappin' their gums by now about the 'new man in town,' so be careful, in the meantime we'll probably be sellin' lots of sewin' goods." As he went to the back room, I could here him muttering, "This could be very good for business."

Ralph Finney was in his early 70s. His family had moved to Lakeland in the 1860s from New England—Vermont, he said. That explained his rather strange accent. He didn't sound like the other people around here. He'd begun to work in the grain and feed store. When the owner died, he bought the place from the heirs. In the mid-'80s (the mid-1880s, that is), he expanded the business to include other merchandise. By the 1890s, "Lakeland Grain and Feed Store" had become "Ralph's Emporium." His wife died in 1902, and he had been living alone in back of the store ever since. Rumor had it that the widow Shelby was sweet on him, but Ralph apparently liked the quiet life of the bachelor. But Ralph had a lot of respect for Agnes Shelby and trusted her judgment in many things. If Mrs. Shelby had set her cap for Ralph, it was very subtle.

Charles Henry

Around one o'clock, the door opened. Rose Fowkes was back.

"It's no use, Jon," said Frances. "You can rant and rave and scream all you want. You can kick down doors; kick the whole house down for all I care. It's none of your business, none of your concern, nothing for you to worry about."

"Not my concern.............not my concern," fumed Jon; then he softened a bit and sat on the bed. "Darling, you're my concern, I want to help you, I want you to be happy."

"You really want to make me happy? You really want to make me happy? Then go away and let me sleep," and she began sobbing softly into her pillow. Jon was all set to say more, but instead slowly got up from the bed; by this time Iris and Edward were at the fallen bedroom door.

"Edward, see to this, get it fixed." "Yes, sir" was Edward's stoic reply.

"Iris, I'm going to the studio and talk to Tony Mann, maybe I can get some answers from him and make some sense out of this mess."

"I'll go with you," said Iris. "You're in no condition to drive in this state of mind."

Jon Hall was not a violent man. He was actually very pleasant and easygoing. Despite her great beauty, personality, and popularity, Frances had never given Jon any cause for worry. Jon felt as if his world was crumbling; he didn't want to think the worst of Frances, but all of this mystery was tearing him up inside.

The drive to L.A. was quiet. Cooling off a bit, Jon was beginning to feel embarrassed about the bedroom door incident. Iris was quiet, not because she was angry, but because she was afraid she would let more of the cat out of the bag, inadvertently. The cat's head and shoulders were already out of the bag. Iris was going to do her best to keep the hind legs and the tail IN the bag. She knew that director Anthony Mann didn't know anything, but at least this got Jon out of the house and away from Frances for awhile. She drove slower than usual, on purpose.

Arriving on the set, Tony Mann greeted Jon warmly. Tony and the films editor were going over some scenes and editing them for the finished product of *The Bamboo Blond*. "B" movies were usually on a tight schedule, so Mann was going to be a step ahead.

Will I Ever Know

They still hadn't shot the final scene yet, and he was thinking about doing the first airport scene over again, where Capt. Ransom's parents are seeing him off.

Jon got right to the point. "Tony, what do you know about a guy named Chad who Frances seems to be very fond of?"

"Gee, Jon, I don't know, the other day this jasper all of a sudden shows up on the set, Frances says he's an old friend, then asks for a week off."

"An old friend?"

"That's right," replied Tony, "she said, 'He's an old friend of ours,' I think that's what she said."

"I don't know anyone named Chad, never have. Listen, if he came on the lot by himself, he would have had to sign in at the gate, right?"

"Yes," said Tony, "they should have a record at the gate and, oh, one other thing, the other day Frances dropped in to see me with this Chad character, and he said a weird thing."

"What was it?" asked Jon. Iris stiffened.

"He gave us an ending for the movie, the same one we had just agreed on a few days ago. How did he know that?"

"I'm going out to the gate, thanks, Tony." Iris, remaining quiet, went with him. They left Tony shaking his head and saying to himself, "Who the hell is that guy anyway?"

"Hello again, Mr. Henson," said Rose.

"Good afternoon, Miss Fowkes, what can I do for you?"

"I forgot I needed some thread and some sewing needles, could you help me?" Ralph was right; something told me we were going to sell a lot of sewing materials.

She picked out some spools of different-colored thread, a packet of needles, and two yards of material, in dark green.

"I make most of my own clothes, Mr. Henson, so much cheaper. I'm very thrifty. And I'm quite a cook, too."

"Oh, really" was my short reply, wishing she would just pay her bill and leave.

As I wrapped the goods, Rose leaned over the counter and in a very soft voice, said, "Mr. Henson, the church is having a social next Saturday afternoon. Why don't you accompany me, you can meet many of the town folk, it will be lots of fun. We'll have a hymn sing, games, and lots and lots of food."

Now what, Chad? Now what? If I say no, it might cause suspicion; if I say yes, it will definitely give Rose the wrong impression, and open myself up for endless questions about my background, etc.

"Listen, Miss Fowkes," I said, "I. . . "

Alone in her bedroom, Frances cried until she couldn't cry anymore. Dora entered the room.

"Can I get you anything, miss?" "No thank you, Dora, I just want to be alone."

Frances was angry, not with Jon—he had done nothing—but his unexpected return only muddied the waters more. She was angry at the fates who had given her this dream, through "Will I Ever Know," and had so cruelly and abruptly snatched it away from her.

"Will I Ever Know"—ha, thought Frances, more like "I'll Never Know." Then she thought, No, that's not right, I did know, even if it was only briefly. I did know . . . I did know! The problem was that she wanted it back; oh, how she wanted it back. Her aching heart was broken. Nothing or no one could console her.

Jon and Iris were at the front gate of RKO studios. Jon said, "Gus, can I see the log for Sept. 17th? I'm looking for someone who was here on that date visiting."

"Sure, Mr. Hall, I'll find it for you," said Gus, the security guard. "It's right under here."

Will I Ever Know

Reaching under the desk, Gus pulled out a stack of papers ready to be filed. September 17th's log was almost on the top.

Iris and Jon began looking through the list, Iris knowing that they wouldn't find my name anywhere because I didn't sign in, I "dropped" in.

Jon was getting more frustrated by the minute, as what he was looking for wasn't there.

"Are you sure it was the 17th, Iris? His name isn't here."

"Oh yes," said Iris, "it was definitely the 17th, that's when Tony declared the week off that Frances asked for."

"Well, let's check the 14th, the 15th, and the 16th, can we, Gus?"

"Sure, Mr. Hall, no trouble," and Gus got him the sign-in sheets for those days. Still no luck; no one named "Chad anything" had signed the registers.

"He must have snuck in then," said Jon.

"No, Mr. Hall, that's not possible, no one gets by this desk without signing in and getting a pass. Security has been really tight since the war started, still is even though the war is over."

"How did he do it then?" said Jon in exasperation. "Is he a magician?"

"Jon, let's go," said Iris, lightly grabbing his arm. "Just forget it, he's gone."

Not about to give up, Jon said, "Let's go see Bob Hope, he's close with Fran, he'll know something." Iris rolled her eyes, but was glad Jon wasn't going back home just yet. Although she feared what Hope might say, she was sure he didn't know the whole story.

"Thanks for your trouble, Gus," said Jon. "No problem, Mr. Hall, best to the Mrs., take care, Miss Adrian." And they were off to NBC.

"Miss Fowkes," I said, "I'd be honored to escort you to the church social."

Rose brightened. "Why, Mr. Henson, I'm delighted, you may call for me next Saturday at

3:30." She quickly wrote her address down on a small piece of paper. "357 Elm Street," she said, "it's just around the corner." She handed me the piece of paper and I put it in my shirt pocket.

"Good day to you, sir," she said as she left the store.

"And to you," I said. As she left, I hoped I had done the right thing. I didn't really want to go—I wanted to keep a low profile—but I guess that wasn't possible in this town.

A few minutes later the door opened, and in walked a slightly-past-middle-age, heavy-set lady with a much younger, much more overweight version of herself.

"Good afternoon," she chimed, "I'm Eula Bunce and this is my daughter, Alta May." "How do you do, Mrs. Bunce, Alta May, I'm Chad Henson."

"How do you do, Mr. Henson," said Mrs. Bunce. Alta May was giggling nervously; the only thing she could manage was "Oh, Mr. Henson, hee hee hee hee hee." Mrs. Bunce continued, "So nice to have a young man again in the store, Mr. Henson. I need some spools of thread, and a dress pattern."

"Right this way, Mrs. Bunce," I said, thinking that there would soon be a well-worn path over to the sewing area. "We have some new patterns that just came in from New York."

"Come, come, Alta May," said Mrs. Bunce. More giggles from Alta May.

They spent quite a bit of time looking everything over. They selected several spools of thread and two dress patterns. I rang them up. "That'll be 78¢, Mrs. Bunce."

"Really?" she said. "My, my, prices keep going up every day." She paid me and I gave her the change.

"Oh, by the way, Mr. Henson." Here it comes, I thought. "The church is having a social next Saturday afternoon, and it just so happens that Alta May is without an escort. It would be soooo lovely if you would be her escort." I looked at Alta May, who by this time was as red as the tomatoes in the barrel, and still giggling. "Wouldn't you like that, Alta May?" she said. "Hee hee hee hee" was Alta May's reply.

Now feeling relieved and thankful for Rose Fowkes' invitation, I said, "I'm sorry, ladies, but I've committed to escorting Miss Rose Fowkes to the social."

"Rose Fowkes," harumphed Mrs. Bunce, "well, that is unfortunate, perhaps some other time then."

"Perhaps," I said.

"Come, Alta May, we must be going."

"Bye, ladies," I said. As they were going out the door, I heard Mrs. Bunce say, "I knew we should have come in earlier, if you weren't so busy feeding your face all the time." From a distance I heard, faintly, "hee hee hee hee."

Iris and Jon were sitting in Bob Hope's office. Bob was seated behind a large oak desk. Jon was smoking a cigarette. Bob's office was large and airy with lots of pictures of stars he had worked with lining the walls. Jon got up and started pacing.

"Bob, I'll get right to the point. What do you know about this Chad uh………"
"Henson," chimed in Iris. "Yes," said Jon, "this Chad Henson character."

"Not much," said Bob. "Frances brought him to the USO benefit and our show, said he was a friend of yours—that is, both of you."

Jon ran his fingers through his hair and snuffed out the cigarette angrily in the ashtray on Bob's desk.

"Dammit, Bob, I never heard of a Chad Henson, and Frances has never in nine years mentioned a Chad Henson."

"He seemed like a nice enough sort," continued Bob uneasily. "I sat next to him for the first part of the USO show. I remember when Frances sang 'At Last,' she thr……………." "UMMMHUMMMMMMMP" went Iris, and Bob hesitated, looking perplexedly at her. He was about to say, "she threw him a kiss," but instead, Bob said, "ah, thhh-awed out, beautifully. It was so cold in there, but our trooper Frances really thawed out, yes sir, Frances had been complaining of how cold it was in the theater, she was afraid her voice would be as frozen as an iceberg, but she turned it into a hot number, yes sireeeeee."

Charles Henry

"Bob, don't patronize me. I know that you and Frances are really good friends. Your loyalty is with Frances and I understand that. All of you are trying to keep the obvious from me. The truth is I've lost her, much of it is my fault, I know. Much of it is equally our fault. We are both so busy, flying here and there. We've drifted apart. Honestly, if it weren't for the paycheck I'd walk away from all of this acting and Hollywood crap. I'm going back to the house and try to build some bridges. He's gone, apparently, hopefully for good. Maybe I can help her forget him. Thank you, Bob, we'll be seeing you."

"Listen, Jackson, tell Frances I send her my best. I hope she's feeling better. Tell her to take some time off. I'll line up a guest vocalist for next week."

"Thanks, Bob, you're a good friend, I'll tell her," said Jon. "Thanks, Bob, catch ya later," said Iris with a wink.

She took Jon's arm as they left the office. Bob gave a huge sigh and sat down at his desk.

"We're going back to the house," said Jon. "I'm going to question Dora and Edward. They must know something."

"Jon, they don't know anything, you know what a low profile they keep."

"You're right," sighed Jon, "they spend most of their time with her, they're very loyal, I won't get anything out of them. Probably scare poor Dora out of her wits."

Iris gave a sigh of relief. "I'm going to try and fix this, if it can be fixed. No more shouting, ranting, or raving. I hope Fran and I can work this out."

"Now you're talking," said Iris. "Do you want me to leave?"

"I wish you would stay, for a couple of days at least, kind of keep both of us in check."

"You got it, Jon, I'd be glad to, you know you and Frances is like family to me."
"We love you too," said Jon, and he squeezed Iris's hand.

Chapter 40

I Find Out More About Rose/ Iris Spills More of the Beans

The day went on with more younger and older women stopping in at the store and dropping broad hints about the church social. They each bought something at least, which made Ralph very happy. At the end of the day, I asked Ralph about Rose Fowkes. Since I was going to the social with her next week, I wanted to know something about her so we could talk mostly about HER and keep the focus off of me.

"Rose came here 'bout three year ago, fresh outta college, and took the teacher job over to the school. She's attractive, not a beauty, but passable. Young Odell Perkins was sweet on her for awhile, but nothin' come of it. She's involved with the church, teaches Sunday school to the little ones. Came from somewhere around Tampa, I think. Keeps to herself mostly. Goes back home in the summer when school's out. Think she took a cruise a coupla summers ago. That's about all I know," said Ralph.

That wasn't much to go on, but I was hoping it was enough to keep the conversation going next Saturday. I was already having second thoughts about going to the social. Maybe the professor would blink me to another year before next Saturday.

My main concern was Frances; I had seen the look of terror and panic in her eyes before I'd "faded out." What had Prof. Von Schlaban done to her? What had I done to her? I had burst into her life, which had been very happy, very successful. A great career, a nice home, many wonderful, important friends, a bright future that lay ahead for her. I wasn't totally sure about her marriage, but she and Jon had been together almost ten years. Then, because of the words to a silly old song, I landed, and turned this serene, tranquil life into chaos. The professor's words stung my brain………. "Cosmos into Chaos." I had changed the past. What had I done?……….. What would be the results of what I had done?

Arriving back at the house, it was a different Jon Hall that approached Frances, who was still upstairs in the bedroom. The door had been fixed. Frances, not even realizing there had been two carpenters working, didn't hear the hammering. She was pale, drawn, with a faraway look in her eyes. The song "Will I Ever Know" playing over and over in her head. "SHUT UP SHUT UP DAMMIT SHUT UP," she cried to the musicians in her head. Jon and Iris rushed into the room to find Frances in this agitated state.

Jon rushed over to the bed and threw his arms around her. "What is it, darling?" he whispered. "Who are you telling to shut up?" Frances sobbed into his shoulder. "It's nothing, Jon, nothing at all," she cried. "I'm just so tired."

"How about some tea, dearie," said Iris.

"I don't want anything," said Frances. "I just want to be left alone."

"Frances, dear," said Jon. "I'm so sorry about this morning, yelling and screaming like that, I just lost my head. Please tell me what's wrong, please tell me what I've done wrong. I want to make things right again, I can't stand to see you suffering like this."

Frances looked right at him but somehow right past him. "It's that damn music!!!!!!!!!! Make them STOP!!!!!!!!!" And with that she rushed from the bed into the bathroom, slamming the door. Muffled sobs could be heard coming from behind the door. Jon said, "Iris, we've got to do something, she can't go on like this, she's having a breakdown."

"Jon," said Iris, "sit down, I think it's time you knew the whole truth."

The days went on, and it was getting closer to Saturday night. Rose Fowkes made an appearance each day in the store, buying at least one item each day, and giving me what was I suppose the 1915 version of a "come hither" look.

By Wednesday I was really getting to feel uncomfortable about Saturday. And I was not close to feeling that I would be "plucked" out of 1915 very soon.

Will I Ever Know

Late that Wednesday afternoon, about 5:30, in walked Rose Fowkes. "Good day, Mr. Henson" was Rose's usual greeting.

"Good day to you too, Miss Fowkes" was my usual reply.

"Lovely day, isn't it, Mr. Henson?"

"Surely is, and I'm glad the workday is almost over, it's been very busy in here."

Rose didn't beat around the bush. "I know it's almost closing time, Mr. Henson, I was wondering if you might walk me to my house, seeing the lateness of the hour and all."

Oh boy, I thought. I felt like I was in a low-budget western with the local "school marm" falling for the strange, mysterious new cowboy in town. I wasn't interested in the least in Rose Fowkes, and I surely wasn't interested in walking her home or having any "home-made fudge" or "homemade cookies," which I was sure would be the next phase of this "seduction."

Despite the voices in my head screaming "NOOOOOOOOOOOOOOOOO!" my reply was "I'd be delighted, Miss Fowkes, just let me total up and clear the register." Despite the head voices, I felt it would be scandalous in 1915 for a "gentleman" to refuse to accompany a lady to her home with dusk approaching.

"Take your time, Mr. Henson, don't let me rush you."

Ralph came in from the back. "Evenin', Miss Fowkes," he said. "Good evening, Mr. Finney," said Rose. "I hope you're fine."

"Fit as a fiddle," gloated Ralph, "whatever that means, don't rightly know as I've ever seen a 'fit' fiddle." We all laughed.

"Mr. Finney," said Rose, "you will be closing early next Saturday, won't you, for the church social?"

"Yep, yep, do it every year, I 'spect I'd get run clear out of town if I didn't. The Rev. Markham would send me straight to hell! HaHaHa."

"Oh, I don't know about that, Mr. Finney," Rose replied seriously, "but your new employee is escorting me and we don't want to be late, do we. . . Chad?"

"Uh, why, no, no, of course not" was my embarrassed reply.

"We'll close right at 3," said Mr. Finney. "That should be plenty of time for all of us to git there."

"That will be just fine, then I'll look for you, Chad, about 3:15," said Rose.

"Uh, yes, ma'am," I said. I was really looking forward to making a grand entrance!

"Well, I'm set, everything is done and ready for business in the morning."

"Good night, Miss Fowkes, Chad," said Ralph. "See ya in the bright and early." "Good night" was our choral response, and Ralph locked the door and pulled down the shade.

Rose took my arm as we headed down Kentucky Avenue. Trying to make this as quick as possible I said, "I'm really tired tonight"— (multiple yawns) —"very, very busy today, moving boxes, stocking shelves, and lots and lots of customers."

"Oh, you poor dear" was Rose's response, and I thought I caught the "Why don't you stay and I'll fix you dinner?" look in her eye. But no such invitation was forthcoming, much to my relief. After all, it was 1915 and no proper single woman would entertain a "young single gentleman" in her home, alone, especially the "school marm." If word got around she'd probably be condemned by the town council, lose her job, and be ridden out of town on a rail.........with me. Rose was babbling on about something or other, but my mind was back in 1945 wondering about Frances, loving Frances.

"Well, here we are," said Rose. "I'm renting this cottage from Mr. Odell Perkins Sr. He handles the real estate in Lakeland."

"Very nice looking place, Rose, oop, will you look at the time, I must go, Mrs. Shelby has dinner on the table at 6:30 sharp."

"That's too bad, I was hoping we might have a cup of tea on the front porch and you could sit awhile."

Will I Ever Know

"Uh, why, maybe some other time, I do need to get going. Good night, Miss Fowkes."

"Good night to you too…….. Chad," said Rose as I scurried away. She was now getting comfortable in using my first name. The noose was tightening.

"I'm going to tell you what I know," said Iris to Jon, "please don't interrupt, I'll try to answer your questions later."

"It started Sept 17th, Frances doing a scene in *The Bamboo Blond* when all of a sudden, out of nowhere, in 'dropped' this guy Chad Henson."

She then recounted how I just dropped in, said I was from the future, 2007. That I showed Frances a scrapbook full of pictures of her all the way up to the turn of the century. That I was intoxicated by the words to "Will I Ever Know," and that Frances has the same fascination for the song. Iris told him how she'd investigated me and came up with a felon named "Hanson" instead of "Henson." She told him about the picnic, the clearing of my name, the USO show, the party at the Brown Derby, and the Hope show, and that I had just "faded" away backstage while Frances sang "You'll Never Know."

Jon leaned back in the chair. "That's quite a story," sighed Jon. "I can believe everything except this time travel nonsense."

"But, Jon," said Iris, "how do you explain the pictures of Frances in the scrapbook from the '50s, '60s, '70s, '80s, '90s?"

"Oh, that's not hard to figure out," said Jon. "He took some pictures to a photographer and had them touched up. It's not hard to alter a photograph. This guy worked up a fantastic scheme."

"Alright, Jon, but how do you explain his disappearance? He said the owner of the Time Machine was doing his best to bring him back to 2007. Chad just vanished before our eyes!"

"An old magician's trick," said Jon, "all done with mirrors."

"And that song," said Jon, "I haven't heard it in years." "The moment that I see him I will know him, no matter how impossible it seems. I know just what he'll do, I know just what he'll say, we have met before in dreams," said Iris, quoting the words from the song.

Charles Henry

"And that's what started all of this, some old cliché from an old song? I can't believe Frances is that naïve. This guy picks up some sheet music or the record and builds a whole racket out of it?"

"Well," said Iris, "I believe him, I don't understand it, but I believe him. I was very skeptical at first but I seen the way they look at each other."

"Rubbish," said Jon. "I'm going to try and to talk to her again."

"Be careful Jon, don't upset her any further, she's in a very fra-gile state," said Iris.

"I know" said Jon, "I'll be very careful."

With that, the bathroom door opened and in walked Frances................

Chapter 41
Realization

Back at Mrs. Shelby's we had dinner, fried chicken, and I was really totally exhausted more from the Rose Fowkes' incident than anything, but I really had worked hard that day so I decided to go right to bed, at 7:45 p.m.

No wonder they worked such long hours in 1915. There was nothing else to do; no radio, no TV. Movies were still a novelty. I didn't have my scrapbook; it was in the closet in Frances' guest room. I hoped Jon Hall wouldn't find it.

I was up before dawn the next day. I'd slept restlessly, dreaming of Frances, and dreaming of having Rose Fowkes showing me off at the social. Seeing Frances in the distance. I would run toward her, but she kept moving farther and farther away. I woke up in a cold sweat. I showered, shaved, and dressed. I sat outside on the porch to wait for breakfast.

"Mr. Henson," called Mrs. Shelby, "breakfast." I ate breakfast with my two taciturn partners, Mrs. Shelby fluttering around in the background, little Peaches circling my chair. She had found a sucker, and she knew it as I fed her small bits of bacon.

Finishing breakfast, I cheerily said, "Good day, everybody," and I was off to work.

As I headed down Kentucky Avenue, that woman with the screaming baby came towards me. What I'd thought was a lovely child had become an annoyance. Every time I saw

Charles Henry

them, the kid was screaming and trying to get out of her stroller. We passed without a word or a glance, except the baby again turned around and was reaching out, wailing to beat the band. The woman had my admiration. I thought, I'd hate to have to deal with that all day long.

Ralph had already opened up the store as I went in and got right to the inventory. It was only 7 o'clock. I had plenty to do until customer time. The parade of "fair damsels" had ceased. Word had obviously gotten around that Rose Fowkes had bagged the "eligible" young man from Ralph's.

At noon, I told Ralph I was going down to Sam's Soda Shop for lunch. In addition to soda and ice cream, they had sandwiches, candy, cards, etc.

Another beautiful day; my mood was better although Frances was on my mind. I continually replayed all of my time with her. The things she said, the things she did, all the things we did together.

I walked into Sam's and sat down at my usual spot at the counter. "What'll you have?" asked Sam. "Grilled cheese and a Coke" was my reply.

"Hey, that's the third time this week," chuckled Sam. "I know," I said in a wry tone, "I'm very cheesy."

I picked up a paper to read while I ate. While waiting for my food, I noticed the lady with the baby paying for some candy and other things. The baby turned toward me, and the screaming, the reaching out, began again.

I couldn't believe how this baby always screamed and held out her arms every time she saw me. Well, at least they were leaving before that screaming got on my nerves again. I settled in to what I hoped would be a peaceful lunch.

Looking at the masthead of the paper, it suddenly hit me. Lakeland—this was Lakeland, Florida, Sept. 1915. Lakeland, Florida. Frances was born in Lakeland, Florida! It was 1915, so she'd be . . . two years old........................ That baby!

"Sam, who is that lady with the baby that just walked out?"

"Her? That's Mrs. Langford and............................. I shot out of the soda shop,

162

spied them going down Kentucky Avenue. . . "FRANCES," I cried. "FRAN-------CES!!!!!!!!!!!!!!!!!!!!!!!!!!"

As I caught up to them, the woman turned, frightened, and said, "H…How do you know my baby's name?"

"FRANCES!" I screamed again. The baby turned to me with arms outstretched………………………………

"Oh, dear GOD, FRANCES!!!!!!!!!!!!!!!!!"…………………………………….

Finis

Cast of Characters

- denotes fictional character
** denotes historical person

Frances Langford 1913-2005**
Glamorous singer/actress from the 1930s to the 1960s. Spent years touring with Bob Hope and the USO shows entertaining the troops all over the world during WWII, Korea, and Vietnam. Nicknames include "The Dixie Pixie" and "The Florida Thrush." Best remembered for her stunning version of "I'm in the Mood for Love." Her last movie, a cameo appearance, included her playing herself in the 1954 movie *The Glenn Miller Story* and singing "Chattanooga Choo Choo."

Chad Henson*
The obsessed fan in love with Frances Langford. Goes back in time to meet her.

Iris Adrian 1912-1994**
Famous character actress, 1930s into the 1980s. Almost always played the receptionist, phone operator, and wisecracking friend of the female lead. She appeared in scores of films, radio shows, and TV shows.

Ralph Edwards 1913-2005**
Created many popular game shows for radio and TV. One of the most well-known was *Truth or Consequences*, which he hosted. Gained fame on TV with the '50s show *This is Your Life*. Also co-produced the original *People's Court*. Was also a fine comedian appearing in many comedy films of the '40s. Had a prominent role in Frances' movie *The Bamboo Blond*.

Jon Hall 1915-1979**
Frances' first husband. They divorced in 1955. Romantic leading man in adventure films. Most famous today for his early 1950s TV show *Ramar of the Jungle*. Best-known film *The Hurricane*, 1937, directed by John Ford. Committed suicide in 1979 due to a painful illness. He and Frances remained friends after the divorce.

Bob Hope 1903-2003**
Comedian, film star, and star of radio and TV. Famous for his USO tours during WWII, Korea, and Vietnam. Lived to celebrate his 100th birthday.

Supporting Players

Smith Ballew 1902-1984**
Began his career as a radio singer. In the 1930s he became one of the screen's first singing cowboys. Co-starred with Frances Langford in the 1936 movie *Palm Springs*, from which "Will I Ever Know" came from.

Ethel Barrymore 1879-1959**
Along with brothers John and Lionel, formed the royal family of American theater in the 20th century. The stage was her first love but she made many fine films, including *Portrait of Jennie* in 1948. She was Chad Henson's seat partner for part two of the USO VICTORY Benefit.

Humphrey Bogart 1899-1957**
Screen legend known for such classic films as *The Petrified Forest, Casablanca, The*

Maltese Falcon, *The Big Sleep*, and *Key Largo*. He gave Chad directions to Frances' dressing room after the USO VICTORY Benefit.

Alta May Bunce*
Shy daughter of Eula, was hoping Chad would take her to the church social.

Eula Bunce*
Mother of Alta May. Tried to play matchmaker in getting Chad to escort her daughter to the church social.

Justus Campbell*
An ex-GI, he gives Chad a job in his Koffee Korner luncheonette after Frances sends Chad away.

Jack Carson 1910-1963**
Brilliant comedic actor in supporting roles. Perfect foil for Iris Adrian. Appeared in many "B" movies but also made some "A" movies. Made a name for himself on radio in the 40's. Appeared with Iris Adrian and Phil Silvers in a comedy sketch for the USO VICTORY Benefit.

Feliccia Christianson*
Chad's ex-wife, Philadelphia police officer. Moved to Seattle, WA.

Melvin Clark*
Hotel clerk at Chad's hotel. Sells Iris his blazer for $22 so Chad won't look shabby at the USO VICTORY Benefit.

Maxine Duval*
Server at Frances Langford's restaurant in 1995.

Skinnay Ennis 1909-1963**
Famous bandleader of the '30s and '40s. Worked on many radio shows including Bob Hope's. Worked with Frances on "Moonglow" for the Bob Hope show.

Ralph Evinrude 1907-1986**
Frances' second husband.

T. J. Farnsworth*
Manager of a grocery store in 1945 Los Angeles where Chad Hanson worked. Chad Hanson is the man that Iris mistakes for Chad Henson.

Ralph Finney*
Owner of Ralph's Emporium in Lakeland and Chad's boss in 1915.

Rose Fowkes*
27-year-old school teacher in Lakeland. Sweet on Chad, she does her best to get him interested in her in 1915.

Carter Halsey*
Maiître d' at Frances' restaurant in Jensen Beach, FL, 1995

Minerva Larson*
Taciturn rooming house boarder at Agnes Shelby's rooming house in Lakeland, 1915.

Charles Laughton 1899-1962**
Brilliant actor of stage and screen. His many memorable films include *Mutiny on the Bounty* with Clark Gable, 1936, *The Hunchback of Notre Dame*, 1939, *The Paradine Case*, 1947, *Witness for the Prosecution*, 1957, and *Advise and Consent*, 1962. Gave a dramatic reading at the USO VICTORY Benefit show. Showered Frances with accolades after the show. Chad was awestruck.

Anthony Mann 1906-1967**
Director of *The Bamboo Blond*. Gained his experience in 1940s "B" movies. Went on to direct such major motion pictures as *Cimarron*, 1960, and *El Cid*, 1961.

Galen Peabody*
Personnel officer of law firm in Los Angeles where Chad applies for a job in 1945.

Peaches*
Agnes Shelby's cat. Expert food moocher. Had Chad wrapped around her right front paw.

Niko Popodopolous*
Sleazy manager of Chad Hanson's rooming house in Los Angeles, 1945.

Larry Savage*
Chad Henson's best friend in the present. Is very skeptical of the whole Frances Langford thing.

Prof. Ernst Von Schlaban*
Eccentric genius, inventor of the Time Machine. Chad's employer in the present.

Aubrey Scotto 1895-1953**
Early talkies film director. He directed Frances in the movie *Palm Springs*, 1936, where the song "Will I Ever Know" originated.

Agnes Shelby*
Chad's landlady in 1915 Lakeland.

Phil Silvers 1911-1985**
Zany comedian of stage, screen, radio, and TV. His trademark phrase was "Gladaseeya" (Glad to see you). Best remembered for his character Sgt. Bilko in the 1950s television

sitcom *You'll Never Get Rich* (aka *The Phil Silvers Show*).

Sam Spandelman*
Owner and operator of the soda and sandwich shop in Lakeland, 1915.

Harold Stuart 1912-2007**
Frances' third husband. They married in 1994. Went fishing with Frances and Chad in 1995.

Lucius Terry*
Boarder at Agnes Shelby's rooming house in Lakeland, 1915.

Dolph Terwiliger*
Stranger whom Chad bumps into when he arrives in 1915. Directs Chad to Agnes Shelby's rooming house in Lakeland.

Hubert Thompson*
Waiter at the restaurant in Jensen Beach, FL, where Chad arrived in 1995.

Russell Wade 1917-2006**
Co-starred with Frances in *The Bamboo Blond* playing Capt. Patrick Ransom. Appeared in mostly "B" movies in the '40s playing a variety of servicemen. Retired from films in 1948 for a career in business and real estate in Palm Springs.

Songs

"At Last" written by Mack Gordon and Harry Warren 1941

"I'm in the Mood for Love" written by Dorothy Fields and Jimmy McHugh 1935

"Moonglow" written by Hudson, Mills, DeLange 1935

"Sleigh Ride in July" written by Jimmy van Huesen and Johnny Burke 1945

"Will I Ever Know" written by Mack Gordon and Harry Revel 1935

"You Made Me Love You" written by Joe McCarthy and James Monaco 1913

"You'll Never Know" written by Mack Gordon and Harry Warren 1943

Fun Facts of the Forties

Cars: During the war, new cars were manufactured mainly for the Military. Civilians made the best of their old cars.

GM introduced the automatic transmission in 1941. It did not get widespread issuance until 1948. There is a good chance that Frances had manual or stick shift in her car(s).

Fashion: In order to boost morale and show support of the war, women took to styling their hair in innovative ways. Some would part their hair in the middle, creating twin pompadours to form a "V-for-victory" sign. Others had the V on the back or top of the hair.

Because of the shortage of nylons, women would get together and draw black lines down the back of their legs to make it look like they were wearing stockings.

Ankle socks were also popular.

The color of clothing was subdued, and suits and dresses were mostly in solid colors. Off-white was popular for wedding gowns or wedding suits.

Men wore the typical single-breasted or double-breasted suits. Mending became very popular because of rationing, and clothes were worn until they were worn out.

Rationing: Began in the spring of 1942 and wasn't fully ended until 1947. Sugar was one of the items that continued being rationed for a time after the war. Rationing was administered by the OPA (Office of Price Administration).

Some of the items rationed were food products, cloth, wood, metal, gasoline, tires, and auto parts. Some products just weren't made for general consumption as manufacturers turned to making them for the war.

Ration books contained stamps about the size of a regular postage stamp. You had to have stamps to buy the goods. The stores would post weekly how much of a certain item you could buy that week, so you used your stamps accordingly. The system was designed so everyone could get some of what they needed while keeping prices reasonable.

Slang:

Alligator: swing dancers or fans

Cast an eyeball: look around

Dig: like

Hep cats: swing music lovers, dancers male

Hep kittens: swing music lovers, dancers female

High hat you: snub, ignore, disrespect

Shag: an original pursuit

Smooth: good, agreeable

Threads: clothes

Togged to the bricks: wearing one's best clothes

Victory gardens: Because of the rationing of food products, the government encouraged citizens to grow their own vegetables. Nearly 20 million Americans responded. They planted in their backyard, in vacant lots, even on city rooftops, contributing mightily to the war effort.

Printed in the United States
203798BV00004B/1-20/P